DOWNSIZED

a down-sized novel

James A. Booker

PORTLAND • OREGON
INKWATERPRESS.COM

DOWNSIZED

1

The May sky was overcast as Martin Bradley pulled into the parking lot. The sign on the large building in front of him read "Argus Electric Company." The company manufactured electrical components for the automobile industry. The previous day had been Martin's last working day. He had waited until Saturday to finish collecting his personal belongings. He had been a production manager there for nineteen years, but now he was just another victim of the economic slump. At age 58, it appeared that his working days were over. Prospects for finding another job within the range of his expertise were slim to none.

It took him less than two hours to finish clearing his former office. The only other people in the building were the cleaning crew. Soon they would be cleaning his empty office, making it ready for someone younger and more cost-efficient. With his task finished, he returned to his car, loaded it with the remainder of his belongings, and drove away from Argus for the last time.

It rather surprised him that he felt no nostalgia or resentment toward the company. It had provided him with a comfortable income and good benefits for nineteen years, and the separation package was generous. He was simply one of the middle managers who had become expendable because of an ailing economy.

Since it was approaching noon, Martin decided to find a place for lunch, more out of habit than hunger. He didn't want to eat much because he had been invited to supper by a former co-worker, Mike Flannigan. He and his wife, Alice, had been sympathetic and supportive ever since Martin received his pink slip. Martin decided on a Subway sandwich and took his time eating it. He still had four hours to kill before going to the Flannigans'. After lunch, he just drove around Omaha for a while. He hadn't been out to Boys' Town in quite a while, so he drove west until he could see the water tower. The sight reminded him of the old movie with Spencer Tracy as his friends' namesake, Father Flanagan. He noticed that the trees had regained their foliage and flowers were blooming in many areas. The signs of verdant renewal helped him to overcome his feeling of depression. Around mid-afternoon he drove home and unloaded his Buick. He took his time preparing to go out again, since he had nothing better to do. As usual, nothing on afternoon TV appealed to him except during football season. At 4:30 he selected a bottle of wine from his stock and left for the Flannigan home.

Martin arrived at the Flannigans' right at the appointed

time. He had always been a stickler for punctuality. He handed Alice the bottle of wine, and she gave him a hug. Their home was small, but comfortable. Their daughter was grown and married, so it was just the two of them.

At first the situation was a little awkward because of Martin's predicament. Alice countered it by asking him questions about his past.

"You were in the Army before you came here, weren't you?" she asked.

"Yes," he replied. "I went in right out of high school. Since I had tinkered with ham radios as a kid, I was assigned to the Signal Corps. They sent me to Fort Monmouth, New Jersey, for specialized training after basic. I had some good assignments in the U.S. and Europe, so I re-enlisted. The Army sent me to warrant officer school, and I came out a chief warrant officer after twenty years. The later assignments weren't so wonderful, though. I spent a year in Korea and one in Vietnam. But I was able to retire at thirty-eight with a pension and several privileges—commissary, PX, VA medical, etc. That's why I moved to a city where I would have easy access to those."

"You got a college degree somewhere in there, didn't you?" Mike asked.

"Right. I attended night school classes through the Army education program whenever I could. It took eleven years, but I finally got it. It's kinda funny. I have a BS degree from the University of Maryland, and I've never been in Maryland."

"Where did you meet Eloise?" Alice asked.

"In Tokyo. I was there on R & R from Vietnam, and

she was there on a tour. She was a school teacher from Indiana and had five years on me. It seemed improbable, but somehow we hit it off, and we started writing to each other. After my tour in Vietnam was over, I went to see her, and we wound up getting married."

"You must have had some good years before she was diagnosed with MS, didn't you?" Alice asked.

"Oh, yeah! It's too bad you never knew her when she was healthy. She was quite a gal. She was no great beauty, and I'm no Cary Grant, but we really had something special going for us. She couldn't have any children, so all of our focus was on each other."

Alice paused before she asked the next line of questions.

"We know how you cared for her as her condition worsened. That must have been a terrible ordeal. How did you manage?"

Martin tried to maintain his military bearing, but he wasn't very successful. He said, "I took care of her for as long as I could while having to go to work. When she required more care, her sister from Indiana came and stayed with her. We kept her at home as long as we could. But the time came when we had to put her in a care facility. It wasn't long after that when it had to be hospice care."

Alice seemed reluctant to continue, but commented, "We know the rest. We attended her memorial service last November."

Mike weighed in for the first time. "I think it's unconscionable for the company to can you right after you'd lost your wife! Talk about a double whammy!"

Martin just shrugged. "It could be worse," he said. "At

least I'm not left destitute. The company's health insurance covered Eloise's massive medical bills. We couldn't go anywhere the last few years because of her condition, and so we didn't spend much. I have my military pension and VA health coverage plus my severance pay. Actually I don't need to find another job. I just need to find something to do. For the past few years I've just been working and taking care of Eloise. Now I don't have either one. Call it early retirement, but I'm too young to sit on a rocking chair on the porch every day."

Alice had a suggestion. "You might consider volunteer work. They always need people. There's the food shelf, Habitat for Humanity, Meals on Wheels, the Salvation Army. There are lots of possibilities."

Mike added, "There are also on-line sites for connecting with other lonely people, but somehow I doubt if you're ready for that."

Martin just cringed.

Alice asked, "Do you have any plans for the immediate future?"

"I've kicked around a few ideas, but it all seems kinda surreal," Martin answered. "I'm out of shape and overweight, so I need to start some kind of physical activity. I've considered the possibility of volunteer work. My church has a connection with Meals on Wheels, so I might work with them. I might do some traveling. There are still a few places I'd like to see. I could also move away. There's not much holding me here. But I don't know where I'd go. I own a pretty decent home here, and I don't relish the prospect of packing up and moving. I moved enough when I was in the Army. As for the on-line dating game, I can't even imagine doing that. I'm not ready for a relationship anyway."

Mike commented, "You know you'll always be welcome to come here for a visit. We're concerned about your future."

"Oh, I'll be all right," Martin replied. "I was alone a lot before I met Eloise. But I appreciate your concern."

Alice ended the discussion by announcing that supper was ready. For the rest of the evening they just made small talk and tried to avoid returning to Martin's situation. He left around nine and drove back to his empty house.

2

The next morning Martin arose early, as usual, and went for a walk. "It's time to unlimber those muscles," he thought. Most of the houses in the neighborhood were similar but not identical to his. It was an older neighborhood about three miles west of downtown Omaha. The houses were fairly large with small front yards and bigger back yards. Few had garages.

As he returned from his walk, Martin gave an appraising look at his home of nineteen years. He and Eloise had bought it as soon as they moved there. Now it was completely paid off, but looking at the house and the yard, it was evident that he had neglected both for the past few years. Caring for an ailing wife and holding a responsible job had absorbed most of his time and energy. Even after Eloise's death, much of his spare time had been devoted to settling her estate, notifying all of the appropriate parties, and writing thank-you notes to all of the people who had contributed to her memorial fund, helped with the memorial service arrangements, or sent flowers. At her request, her body had been cremated, and so there had been no funeral or burial ceremony. There would be no grave to visit, since both of them had rejected the more traditional practice.

After giving the matter some thought, he decided to go to church. His attendance at the local Presbyterian church had waned over the past few years, particularly after Eloise had been unable to join him. But this time, his main purpose was to inquire about the Meals on Wheels program, which the church supported in conjunction with other charitable organizations. The contact person was a rather large woman named Sarah Best, and Martin approached her after the service. She recognized him and expressed her condolences for his double loss. Responding to his inquiry, she said, "Right now we have everyone covered for the daily routes, but with summer coming, we'll need more people to cover the routes for the regulars who are on vacation."

Martin gave her his telephone number and expressed his willingness to participate in the program.

Returning home, Martin took stock of his prospective activities for the immediate future. He had thought about joining a health club, but he had never enjoyed exercising just for the sake of exercising. He preferred doing something constructive that required some exertion. Looking around him, he could see enough work to keep him occupied all summer. The entire house needed cleaning, and several rooms could use a fresh coat of paint. The back yard was already overgrown with weeds, especially where there had once been a garden. Immediately he started to make a list of what he would need to get started: paint, a new lawn mower, a weed whacker, seeds for the garden, and tools to replace the ones which had been loaned and never recovered. A tool shed would also be a good thing to have, but not right away. The plan was starting to take shape. He spent most of the afternoon digging up his old garden plot and discarding the weeds. His legs were sore when he went inside to watch <u>60 Minutes</u>.

The next day, after his walk, he set out with his shopping list and bought the required items. He decided to start with the garden, since it was already May and the weather was favorable. He could work inside under any conditions. During the next two days he cleared the plot of the remaining weeds, tilled it up, and planted beans, lettuce, radishes, and cucumbers. He bought five tomato plants and added them to the plot. By then his back hurt, but he was pleased with his handiwork.

Later that week he received a phone call from Sarah Best. She asked him if he would accompany a regular Meals on Wheels deliverer in order to learn the route so that he could fill in while the latter was on vacation. Martin agreed to do it.

The next day he met Bart Williams and rode with him as he made eight stops. The first was a woman of about ninety who was only able to stay in her home with some outside assistance. The second was an elderly couple in difficult economic circumstances. The third was a man in his sixties who had fallen off his roof and was on disability from his job. The fourth was a woman who was crippled with arthritis. The fifth was another elderly couple. The wife was bed-ridden, and her husband was doing his best to care for her. The sixth was an elderly widower who wanted to talk to them. Bart had learned how to tell lonely people that he had to keep moving to deliver more meals. Martin took note of his technique. There was no time to stop and chat. Number seven consisted of two sisters in their late eighties who were not especially friendly, but seemed to appreciate the hot meals anyway. The last stop was at an apartment occupied by a very small woman who seemed less obviously needy than the others, but whom Bart described as a charity case. After completing the rounds, Bart drove Martin back to the nursing home where he had left his car.

Since he would not be delivering meals until the next week, Martin applied his energy to getting the yard in shape. After he had it all weeded, mowed, and trimmed, he decided to plant a variety of flowers next to the house. Eloise had always loved flowers.

That Saturday he received a phone call from the Flannigans. They were just checking up on him. He assured them that he was all right and staying out of mischief. He also invited them to come over and admire his handiwork. "Just look at the outside," he said. "I haven't even started on the inside yet." He also told them about his delivery job with Meals on Wheels.

Martin's delivery schedule started the following Monday. He drove to the place where the meals were prepared at around eleven. There he received a large insulated bag with the hot meals. That day they were chicken pot pies with an apple cobbler dessert. As he started to make the rounds, he observed that most of the shut-ins were too anxiously focused on their only hot meal of the day to try to initiate a conversation with him. He was therefore able to move quickly down the list. That continued until he reached the last stop. It was the apartment of the "charity case," a woman named Loretta Beach. She was a diminutive woman of about seventy-five who was in no hurry to eat her hot meal. Rather, she seemed starved for conversation. Since she was his last stop, he couldn't honestly tell her that he had to keep moving. She offered him a cup of tea while she told him more than he really wanted to know about her past. He learned that she had been married and divorced a long time ago and had worked as a retail clerk until forced to retire. Now she was confined to her apartment because of a litany of aches and pains. She passed the days by reading romance novels and watching soap operas on television. Her neighbors in the apartment building were all much younger and had neither time nor sympathy for her. Martin nodded obligingly as she talked, then found a lull in her monologue which enabled him to find a way out and leave.

The next three days passed in roughly the same order. By then he knew Loretta's entire life history, and she knew practically nothing about his. On Friday he knocked on her door, braced for another cup of tea and more empty chatter. He was somewhat surprised when she answered the door wearing a bath robe. He was even more surprised, after he had set the food on the table, when she posed a question: "I haven't been able to take a bath in over a month. I can wash my hair and sponge off in the sink, but if I climb into the tub, I can't get back out. Would you help me take a bath?"

Martin was nonplussed. This wasn't part of the bargain. He asked her, "Don't you have a shower?"

"No, just a bath tub."

"Isn't there a female neighbor or acquaintance who could help you?" he asked.

"I don't know the neighbors, and anyway they're always busy. I'd really like for you to help me."

Martin contemplated his options and didn't like any of them. With serious reservations, he said, "Oh, all right. But just this once."

Loretta smiled slightly, then went into the bathroom to turn on the bath water.

"This is a really bad idea," Martin told himself.

After the water was drawn, Loretta removed the bath robe. She seemed totally at ease having a man whom she hardly knew seeing her naked. She was a tiny woman, probably weighing less than a hundred pounds. Her breasts were so small that they barely protruded behind the nipples.

"At least she won't have to worry about them sagging," Martin thought.

She had very little pubic hair. As Martin helped her into the tub, it occurred to him that from the neck down she looked more like a twelve-year-old girl than a seventy-five-year-old woman.

As she eased down into the hot water, Martin said, "If you like, I'll wait outside."

"Oh, please stay here and talk to me," she replied.

Martin shrugged and sat down on the toilet stool cover. As usual, she chatted on about her past while Martin listened. After about ten minutes the water was cooling, and Loretta was ready to climb out.

"This is the part I can't manage," she said.

Martin grasped her under her arms and raised her out of the tub. Then he picked up a bath towel and dried her off. Rather than feeling any kind of sexual arousal, he almost felt as if he were dealing with a child. He had never had a daughter, but he could imagine that it would be similar to this.

When she was dry, Loretta put on her robe. "Oh, that felt good," she said. "I used to take a bath every day."

Martin drained the tub and rinsed it out. He couldn't think of anything intelligent to say.

"Would you like a cup of tea?" Loretta asked.

"No, thank you," he replied. "I really should be going."

"Well, thank you for your assistance. I really appreciate it," she said.

Martin just nodded.

As he drove home, Martin thought, "I don't think I'll discuss this with anyone."

3

During the next week Martin made considerable progress in cleaning his house. He even got the bathrooms painted. The house had three bedrooms, one downstairs and two upstairs. After Eloise's condition had become critical, he had moved into one of the upstairs bedrooms. When his sister-in-law arrived, she occupied the other one. Now he would have to decide what to do with the two extra bedrooms.

Martin also completed his obligation with Meals on Wheels that week. By then he had the routine down, and his deliveries went smoothly and quickly. He always held his breath when he knocked on Loretta Beach's door, but she greeted him fully dressed and made no mention of the bathing episode.

When Bart Williams returned from his vacation, he called Martin to find out if anything unusual had happened.

"No, everything went well," Martin replied. "I made all the deliveries on schedule."

"Did Loretta give you any trouble?" Bart asked.

"No, other than being too chatty. Why do you ask?"

"Would you believe she asked me to help her take a bath once? Of course, I declined," Bart said.

"That must have added a little spice to your routine," Martin commented.

"That was a little more 'spice' than I needed. I referred her problem to one of the female supervisors. I think she went there to help Loretta."

"I suppose that was the way to handle it," Martin replied noncommittally.

"Well, thanks for filling in for me. Maybe we'll meet again."

"That would be good," said Martin for no particular reason.

During the following three weeks, Martin filled in for two more vacationers, but for shorter periods of time. He found the work gratifying, and it also gave him a reason to take a break from his work at home. Soon he would be running out of projects and would have to find something else to do. He considered starting graduate classes at the Omaha branch of the University of Nebraska, but he wasn't sure he wanted to do that. A master's degree wouldn't do him much good, and he could always learn on his own without having to pay tuition.

It was at that point that one telephone call resolved his dilemma. It came from a social worker in Chicago named Diane McDermott.

"Mr. Bradley, you were referred to us by a woman named Jewel Bradley. After learning that her parents were no longer living, she named you as her only known living relative."

Martin drew a sharp breath as Diane McDermott continued.

"She has been arrested for trying to sell crack cocaine to an undercover police officer and is facing a prison sentence. Can you fill me in on the family connection?"

Martin was too shocked to reply for a moment. Finally he responded.

"Jewel is my niece. Her father was my older brother. I was in the military when she was growing up in Kansas City and seldom saw her. My observation was that my brother and his wife had conceived her when they were about forty and had almost given up on having a child. They named her Jewel and showered her with affection. When I saw her, I thought she was a self-indulgent spoiled brat. She was my only niece, but I couldn't even like her."

"We didn't know about the Kansas City connection. Please continue," she said.

"When Jewel was sixteen, she ran away. Her parents tried every avenue to find her, but she had just disappeared. They were devastated. Four years later they both died in a highway accident. Jewel must have had no way to know about it. You say she just found out?"

"Yes. We couldn't tell if she was even upset when we told her. She never changed expression."

"Well, if you're calling to ask if I'll post bail, the answer is no. I hardly know her."

"That isn't the reason I'm calling you," Diane McDermott replied. "Jewel has two children. Twins. A boy and a girl. Nine years old. They're in temporary foster care now, and we're trying to determine what to do with them."

Martin exhaled audibly, then summarized, "Let me see if I have this straight. My niece dropped off the radar screen about fourteen years ago. Now she emerges as a drug dealer, and we have no idea what she was doing the rest of the time. Her name is still Bradley, which suggests that she has never married, but she has two children, who are probably well on their way to becoming juvenile delinquents. Now just what do you expect from me?"

After a pause, Diane continued, "I'd like for you to hear me out. These kids are like nothing you'd expect. It seems that Jewel and her kids lived across the hall from a retired school teacher named Marian Webster. We don't know the exact circumstances of the arrangement, but it appears that Jewel hired Marian Webster to watch the kids when they were about four. As I said, we don't know much about the nature of the arrangement or what Jewel was doing for a living, but the upshot was that Marian Webster found a new career as a teacher when she learned that the kids were exceptionally bright. Jewel declared them home-schooled when the authorities came knocking, and they actually were. It seems that the woman made a retirement project of educating two receptive children. She even taught them to play the piano."

Martin felt somewhat overwhelmed by this information. He still didn't know just what was expected of him, but it certainly held his attention.

Diane continued. "A few weeks ago, Marian Webster collapsed with a heart attack. She was moved to a care facility, where she remains. That left Jewel with a dilemma. Her response was to leave the children alone while she went out. She left the television tuned to the Discovery channel as their only source of companionship. She even removed the channel selector knob so they couldn't change it. When we found them, the only food in the apartment was half a loaf of bread and some peanut butter and jelly. We found out that the children had never been to a doctor or a dentist, had never been to school, and had never even played with other children. We added child neglect to the drug charges against Jewel."

Martin felt a turmoil of emotions. He asked, "Does anyone know who their father is?"

Diane replied, "If Jewel knows, she isn't saying. The paternal block on their birth certificates is left blank. It seems possible that she had multiple partners and doesn't even know who the father of her children is."

It took Martin a moment to respond. "Maybe it's a blessing that her parents didn't live to find out what a mess she made of her life."

"Maybe so," Diane replied, "but we are still left to decide what to do with the children. They deserve better than they've known up to now."

"So you want me to take them. That would solve your problem," Martin said.

"It could be conditional. We'd have a welfare worker in your area monitor the situation. If it doesn't work out, they could be moved into foster care."

Martin drew a deep breath. "I'm probably going to regret this, but I don't see how I can justify ignoring it. I'll try it under your conditions. So what are their names and how do we proceed?"

"Jewel named them Opal and Onyx. She called them her two gems. But Marian Webster nick-named them Minnie and Max. They seem to prefer those names. As for the transfer, we can bring them to you next week. Can you be prepared by then?"

"I guess I'll have to," Martin replied.

"Good. We'll call you when we're ready. There won't be much to bring along. Jewel was behind on her rent, and so the landlord claimed most of her belongings, such as they were. The kids will need new clothes and haircuts. We took them to a doctor and a dentist. They're malnourished and socially inept, but other than that, they're reasonably normal."

With that they concluded the conversation, leaving Martin to wonder what he was in for.

4

With the arrival of the children impending, Martin devoted his attention to preparing the house for them. The main focus was on the two upstairs bedrooms. Each had a twin bed and a closet, but only one had a dresser. He picked one up at a used furniture store. Then he started finding new locations for the accumulation of clutter in the rooms. Some of it went to the basement, and some went to Good Will, including most of Eloise's sewing items. He had already disposed of her clothing and shoes. He decided to wait to shop for groceries until the twins arrived, since he had no idea what they might like to eat. He was also clueless as to what they would bring with them, but speculated that it would not be much. His contact had said that their landlord had claimed the furniture and household items for lack of payment. When he had finished preparing the rooms, he reflected that it had been fortunate timing for him to clean the house.

After he had finished making preparations, Martin called the Flannigans and told them about this latest development. He had a special request for Alice.

"I've never been around children very much. I could really use a resource person to turn to when I need help. May I count on you?"

"Of course," she replied. "I'd be glad to help. One of the first items on the agenda will probably be to buy some new clothes. I'd be more than happy to help you pick out some clothes for your niece."

"I hadn't even thought of that," said Martin. "They'll certainly need some new clothes before school starts."

"Their new case worker will probably help you get them enrolled in their new school," Alice added.

"That will be a new experience for them. They've never been to school—or much of anywhere else, as I understand."

Alice chuckled. "A few weeks ago you were trying to figure out what to do with your free time. I guess you have a project now."

"And how!" Martin replied. "This is going to be a challenge."

"We'll do all we can to help you, but we have confidence in you."

"Thanks. I'm sure I'll be calling you soon," Martin concluded.

+~+

The next evening Martin received another call from Diane McDermott in Chicago.

"We plan to leave early tomorrow morning. We expect to arrive at your place by late afternoon. Are you ready for us?" she asked.

"I'm about as ready as I can be under the circumstances," he replied.

"Good. As I mentioned earlier, the children have been to a doctor and a dentist. I'll give you their shot records. We also got their hair cut. They were pretty shaggy. They don't have many clothes, though, and the ones they have are well worn."

"I was expecting to take them shopping for new clothes," he said.

"That will be another new experience for them. I doubt if they've ever had new clothes. Jewel got theirs from the Salvation Army store."

"I'll take care of that matter," he said. "I've already recruited a fashion advisor."

"Fine," she said. "You should also be aware that they've been on a pretty meager diet, especially since they lost their tutor. She used to feed them. Since she left, the kids have eaten mostly peanut butter and jelly sandwiches. Their stomachs have shrunk, and it will take time for them to adjust to a normal diet. I'd go easy on rich or spicy foods for a while. We took them out to McDonald's and ordered them Happy Meals. They split one and couldn't even finish that. They took the other one along."

"Thanks for the warning. I'll be careful," he said.

"Just one more item. Since they'll be leaving Illinois,

they need a new case worker. In a few days you'll be contacted by Angela DiMarco from Omaha social services. She'll monitor the children's progress until the situation stabilizes."

"I'll take all the help I can get," Martin replied. "This is all new to me."

"I'm sure you'll be just fine. The children have been polite and cooperative with us," she said.

"OK. I'll see you tomorrow then," Martin concluded.

＋〜＋

The next day dragged slowly for Martin. It occurred to him that Diane and her driver would not have eaten supper, and he decided to pick up a big bucket of Kentucky Fried Chicken with cole slaw, mashed potatoes, and gravy. If they decided not to stay, the food would still be good as left-overs. It annoyed him that he felt so nervous.

At around 4:00 p.m. a dark blue van pulled up in front of the house. Diane McDermott got out first and introduced herself to Martin. Then she opened the back door, and the twins emerged. They looked as nervous as Martin felt. He squatted down in order to meet their eye level.

"Hello. I'm your Uncle Martin," he said.

The two nodded shyly.

"What do you want me to call you?" he asked.

"I'm Max," said the boy.

"I'm Minnie," followed the girl.

Martin observed that the boy was slightly taller than his sister and had lighter brown hair. He also had blue eyes, while hers were brown. They barely looked like siblings, let alone twins. They were both wearing faded jeans, old Chicago Cubs T-shirts, and badly worn tennis shoes with no socks.

The driver had already started unloading the plastic bags which contained the children's meager possessions. There were only six.

"Why don't we go inside and see where you're going to live?" Martin suggested. He offered a hand to each child, and they accepted the gesture timidly. Diane and the driver picked up some bags and followed them into the house.

"I hope you'll stay for supper," Martin said to Diane. "I picked up some KFC chicken."

"That would be nice," she replied. "It would also help us make the transition."

Martin gave them a quick tour of the house. The twins seemed the most impressed by the fact that the house had two bathrooms. They had never imagined such a luxury. They seemed less impressed with their bedrooms, since they were nearly empty.

The driver, who was simply introduced as Wally, brought the remaining two bags inside. He had very little to say during their brief stay. Diane tried hard to bridge the awkward gap between Martin and the children. She kept asking them questions, but they replied with the tersest of answers. Finally she turned to Martin and asked him what he planned for them to do the next day. He replied, "First, we'll go grocery shopping. I waited until they arrived to find out what they like to eat. Since I'm retired military, I have commissary privileges. I usually go to Offutt Air Force Base south of here once a month to stock up on lower-priced groceries. After that, we'll just have to see what else we need. A friend has offered to help us shop for clothes."

With that, Minnie's face lit up. "Do you mean we'll get some new clothes?"

"You sure will," Martin replied.

Diane shook her head and said, "You realize, they've never had new clothes. This will be a novelty for them."

Everyone seemed to enjoy the meal, especially the chicken. Martin felt that he had made a wise choice by picking up fried chicken with mashed potatoes and gravy. Nearly everyone likes that.

After they had eaten, Diane and Wally stayed for perhaps another hour while she offered advice and background information. The children took the bags upstairs and started sorting out their meager possessions. Then the two welfare workers from Chicago left to spend the night in a motel, where they had already checked in. Martin was pleased to have received so much useful information.

As soon as they had departed, Martin went upstairs to check on his new charges. They were still unpacking the plastic bags and sorting out the contents. The clothing was all well worn, and the bed sheets were too large for the twin beds. Martin observed that there were no toys or games. There were a few books and just one small photo album.

"You can put your things away tomorrow," he said.

"Why don't we get better acquainted this evening? You probably have some questions for me."

As they went downstairs, Minnie seemed to notice for the first time that there was a piano in the living room.

"Oh, Miss Webster had a piano," she exclaimed. "May we play it?"

"Certainly," Martin replied. "My wife used to play it. I never learned how."

Minnie then lifted the keyboard cover, sat down on the bench, and started to play Beethoven's "Fuer Elise." She seemed upset when she made some mistakes.

"I haven't been able to play since Miss Webster left," she said. "I'm out of practice."

"You can practice here all you want," said Martin. "If you like, we'll find someone to give you music lessons."

Minnie smiled, then turned to her brother. "It's your turn," she said.

Max sat down on the bench and started to play a Scott Joplin tune. He made fewer mistakes than his sister. She seemed to notice that and frowned.

Martin said, "Since we have two musicians here, I'll have the piano tuned and see if we can find someone to continue your lessons."

He had instinctively learned not to talk down to the children, since they seemed to talk more like miniature adults than children.

After that, they sat in the living room, where he answered their questions. They wanted to know about his wife and how he was related to them. He was amazed by the intelligence of their questions.

"So you're actually our great uncle," said Max. "We thought you seemed a little too old to be our uncle."

Martin was too amused by the comment to feel offended. "That's right," he said. "Your mother is my niece. But you can still call me Uncle Martin unless you have a better name for me."

The twins looked at each other and nodded. "We think you look like an Uncle Martin," said Max.

Martin smiled. Then he asked, "What time do you usually go to bed?"

"Around nine," answered Minnie.

"And what do you like for breakfast?" asked Martin.

The two seemed stumped for an answer. "We didn't eat breakfast," said Max.

"Well, here we eat breakfast," said Martin. "We'll try pancakes tomorrow and see how you like that."

The expressions on their faces indicated that they didn't know what pancakes were.

At nine o'clock Martin led the pair upstairs. They had received tooth brushes from the dentist, and so they dutifully brushed their teeth. When Martin asked them if they had pajamas, they told him that they had always slept in their underwear. Since they seemed not to require any further assistance, he left them to put themselves to bed.

After he had read the newspaper and watched the late news, he decided to look in on the children. Both of their bedroom doors were open. As he looked in on Minnie, he was startled to see that her bed was empty. Hurrying to Max's room, he was both relieved and surprised to see both of them asleep in Max's bed.

Martin's initial reaction was quickly replaced by the realization that the two had never had separate beds before. He thought, "If they were fourteen, I'd have reason to be concerned, but at nine, I don't see a problem."

5

The next morning, a Friday, Martin arose early and mixed up batter for pancakes. The children came down at about seven. They hadn't tried to comb their hair yet and therefore looked even more bedraggled than they had the previous evening. Martin ignored their disheveled appearance and wished them a good morning.

"Would you like milk or orange juice while I fry the first batch of pancakes?" he asked.

The twins looked somewhat bewildered at the question, but Minnie replied, "I'd like some orange juice, please."

"So would I," echoed Max.

Martin poured two small glasses of orange juice, then turned his attention to the pancakes.

"We're going grocery shopping this morning," he announced. "What would you like to get?"

The two looked at each other in amazement. Finally

Max replied, "Anything but peanut butter and jelly sandwiches."

"Is there anything that you really dislike?" Martin asked.

Again they looked at each other and Minnie replied, "We've never even thought about that. We just ate whatever was there. It was either that or go hungry."

Martin was still trying to grasp the abominable conditions under which these children had lived. Finally he asked, "When was the last time you went to a grocery store?"

The delayed response was, "Mama left us at home when she bought groceries. We don't remember ever going along."

By then the first batch of pancakes was ready, and Martin showed them how to put syrup on them. The menu was an instant hit. They ate three small pancakes apiece.

"Can we have more of these tomorrow?" asked Max.

"You can have pancakes as often as you like," Martin replied. "You might want to try something else soon, though."

❧

After breakfast, Martin combed the children's hair and strapped them into the back seat of his Buick. Then he drove south to Offutt Air Force Base. The sticker on his windshield allowed him to enter the base past the guard with no questions asked. His first destination was the commissary. As they left the car, he cautioned the twins, "Stay with me! This is a big place, and you could get lost."

As they entered the building, the two were over-whelmed by the number and variety of items on display. Martin had to remind himself constantly that these two nine-year-olds had spent most of their young lives in a run-down apartment building. Nearly everything would be a novelty to them.

Martin hadn't made a list, and so he just picked out items as the mood struck him. He was somewhat sur-prised that the twins didn't ask him to buy anything in particular. It occurred to him that they probably didn't know what most of the items were.

` When they reached the meat department, Martin bought a big supply of hamburger, hot dogs, bratwurst, and chicken. He recalled reading that young children don't share adults' passion for steaks and chops, since they have trouble chewing them.

By the time they reached the check-out station, they had well over a hundred dollars worth of groceries. Even at that, it was considerably less than it would have cost at a grocery store.

After loading their purchases and the children into the Buick, Martin then drove to the PX. There he bought a grill, a large bag of briquets, and an electric fire starter. He hadn't grilled in several years, but now he looked forward to doing it again.

Driving home, the children had little to say, and so Martin turned on the radio. The station was playing some older popular music. Glancing in the rear view mirror,

Martin could see that the twins were much more interested in the unfamiliar music than they were the unremarkable landscape.

It was nearly noon when they reached his home. The twins dutifully helped him carry their purchases into the house. After he had taken care of the perishable groceries, he started to prepare lunch. With so little time to prepare, he decided to heat up some chicken noodle soup. As an afterthought, he turned on the television set so that the twins could watch something while he prepared lunch. As it turned out, there was a teen tournament of <u>Jeopardy</u> in progress. Martin could hear the sound from the kitchen. He heard Alex Trebek announce: "The first contestant has chosen world capitals."

The first "response" was Helsinki.

Max hollered, "Finland!"

The second "response" was Amman.

Minnie yelled, "Jordan!"

They were ahead of the contestants, who were required to frame their responses in the form of questions.

Then one of the contestants changed the category to planets. The board lit up, and Alex Trebek read, "The deities for whom most of the planets were named."

"Roman gods!" was Minnie's vocal response.

The next cue was a planet named for a god of the sea.

"Neptune!" replied Max loudly.

Martin was so absorbed in the contest that he suddenly realized that the soup was boiling. He quickly moved to turn off the heat.

The next contestant who answered correctly changed

the category to the Beatles. The TV contestants ran the category while the twins remained silent. They obviously knew nothing about the Beatles.

The next category was famous historical dates. The first clue was 1865.

"End of the Civil War," said Max.

"...and the assassination of President Lincoln," added Minnie.

The next was 1588.

"Defeat of the Spanish armada!" they shouted in unison.

The last contestant to answer correctly switched to famous movie roles. Again the twins were silent.

After the program was over, Martin dished up the soup and called the children to the kitchen table. As they were eating, Martin asked them, "Why didn't you frame your responses to the clues in the form of a question, like the contestants?"

Max shrugged. "Because it doesn't make any sense to us," he said.

Martin drew a deep breath. As unlikely as it seemed, these neglected children had accidentally acquired a unique early education which had stimulated their capacities to absorb it. In short, he had been entrusted with the care of two budding geniuses. Martin tried to recall what Jewel had been like as a child. He couldn't remember anything brilliant about her other than her name. So who was their father? Despite his best efforts, Martin couldn't picture Jewel hooking up with an Einstein.

✛

That afternoon Martin took the twins to a nearby park, where they walked for about an hour. He explained to them the importance of exercise. They had never had any and were probably less interested in it than simply the opportunity to be outside. When he took them back home, he showed them his garden and assigned responsibilities to each of them. They soon came to realize that they would be expected to carry a share of the load.

When the newspaper came, he looked at the ads, contrary to his custom. Penney's was having a sale, as usual, but this time they were trying to get rid of their summer stock in order to make room for their back-to-school line. Martin called Alice and asked her if she would have time to help him buy a new wardrobe for Minnie. She said that she would be only too happy to oblige.

✛

The next morning, after another pancake breakfast, Martin and the twins met Alice at Penney's. After she had been properly introduced, she took Minnie to the girls' department while Martin took Max to the boys' section of the store. The object was to buy just enough clothing to get them through the warmer part of the year. But even that required a considerable amount of shopping. What few clothes they had were both worn out and too small. They would need pajamas, all new underwear, new jeans and shirts, socks, and casual shoes as well as "dress-up" outfits. Alice surprised Minnie by selecting a pretty blue dress for her. When she tried it on and looked in the mirror, she was speechless. She had never dreamed of such finery.

They met at the designated counter, and Martin took out his credit card to pay for their purchases. He tried not to look too surprised when he saw the total. Even with the discounts, it had been an expensive outing. After that, they ate an early lunch at a food court in the mall, and Alice left them.

By the time they returned home, it was too warm for outside activities. Martin helped the twins put their new clothes in the closets and the chests of drawers. Most of their old clothing went into the trash barrel.

Minnie asked, "When can I wear my new dress?"

"We'll go to church tomorrow, and you can show it off," Martin replied.

Martin realized that going to church would be another new experience for the children. It hardly surprised him that religion had not been a part of Jewel's life.

At around five he started the grill and prepared hamburgers and salad. His efforts were rewarded by an affirmative response from his new family.

After supper they watched a Disney movie on television together, and by then it was close to bedtime. Martin said to them, "You should take a bath or a shower. It's kind of a Saturday night tradition. Will you need some help, or can you manage by yourselves?"

Max replied, "We can do it by ourselves. We're used to that."

"All right," said Martin. "Then you can try on those new pajamas."

The twins went upstairs, and Martin sat down in front of the television to watch something more appropriate for his age.

After about half an hour, he started to wonder about his charges. They should have been finished by then, he thought. He climbed the stairs and saw that the bathroom door was half open. As he peeked inside, he could see the two of them in the bath tub together.

"This is going to be interesting," he thought, but he decided not to make an issue of it and simply went back downstairs.

A few minutes later the twins came downstairs wearing their new pajamas.

"We came to say good-night," said Minnie.

"We also want to thank you for the new clothes," said Max.

"You're entirely welcome," replied Martin. "But would it be too much to ask for a good-night hug?"

The twins responded enthusiastically, leaving their great uncle with the most emotional feeling he had had in a long time.

6

The next day Martin awoke to a bright, sunny Sunday morning. He took a quick shower in the downstairs bathroom, then set about preparing breakfast. This time he decided to fry scrambled eggs and sausages. He had everything ready by the time the twins came down. They were wearing some of their new casual clothes. Actually they didn't have much choice, because Martin had thrown out nearly all of the old ones, salvaging only one set apiece for working in the garden. He poured each of them a glass of milk, but he preferred coffee for breakfast. Any doubts he may have had about their taste for eggs was quickly dispelled. The two cleaned up their plates and drank their milk. He noticed that neither of them tried to talk much while they were eating. It was obvious that they liked their new diet. It strained Martin's imagination to think what their former menus had been.

After they had eaten, the two dutifully put their dishes

and glasses into the dishwasher. Martin was trying right from the start to give them some simple responsibilities. They still had over an hour until time to go to church, so he retrieved the newspaper from the front porch. He gave the twins the comics while he looked at the front section. Minnie started to play the piano while Max read the funnies, then they switched. There never seemed to be any friction between the two. It was as if they had organized their own little private existence to the benefit of both.

Soon it was time to get ready for church. While Martin was dressing, Max put on his new dress pants and shirt while Minnie donned her new blue dress. After Martin had combed their hair, they left for church.

The twins looked unsure of themselves as they entered the church. This was another new experience for them. Martin introduced them to some of the people there, all of whom expressed surprise at his new family. Martin looked for some other children, but the few who were there were either considerably older or younger than the twins.

When Martin saw Sarah Best, he introduced the twins to her. The encounter gave him an opportunity to explain that he would be unable to deliver Meals on Wheels until the children were in school. She seemed to understand.

The children's subdued demeanors changed abruptly when the organist began to play the prelude. Here was another first. They had never heard a pipe organ. They could see that it looked something like a piano, but it was much more complex.

"Can we see it up close?" asked Minnie.

"After the service is over," Martin replied.

The children sat patiently through the hour-long service, but predictably they were mystified by the proceedings. They had no frame of reference for any of it. They could only relate to the organ music, which seemed almost magical to them.

After the service, they waited for the congregation to clear out past them, then they approached the organ. The organist was a woman of about thirty-five. She was just concluding the postlude when they reached her. Martin didn't know her personally, so he introduced himself and the twins to her. She replied that her name was Belle Hoskins.

"This is the first time the children have ever heard an organ," said Martin. "They've had some piano lessons and seem to have considerable aptitude. I have an old piano and would like to arrange for them to take lessons again. My piano would need tuning, though."

"I still give a few lessons," said the organist. "Maybe we can work something out. I can also recommend a piano tuner."

Martin turned to the children. "What would you think of that?" he asked.

The expressions on their faces said it all.

After a brief discussion, they agreed on weekly sessions at Belle's home. She also gave Martin the name of a piano tuner.

As they drove toward home, Minnie asked, "Do you think we could learn to play that organ some day?"

Martin smiled and said, "I think you could learn just about anything if you really wanted to."

✦

That afternoon it was too hot and sultry for them to do much outside. Martin decided that it was time for him to introduce the twins to his specialty—electronics. He opened the cabinet below the television set and revealed a state-of-the-art home entertainment system. He also had a fairly new computer. He started slowly to show them how each feature functioned, but they picked it all up rapidly. At the end of the first session, he selected a CD which he predicted that they would like. It was a restored 1937 recording of George Gershwin's "Rhapsody in Blue" as performed by the Paul Whiteman orchestra with Oscar Levant at the piano. The twins listened with rapt attention. They were just starting to realize the upper limits of keyboard playing.

"Do you suppose we could ever play like that?" Max asked.

"With enough practice, anything is possible," Martin replied.

After that, there was nearly always music in the house as the children discovered Eloise's keyboard recordings of Bach, Liszt, Chopin, and Rachmaninov. They could hardly wait to resume their piano lessons.

✦

The next morning after breakfast and their walk, the phone rang. It was Angela DiMarco, the children's new case worker. She wanted to arrange a meeting with them. Since Martin had no firm plans, they agreed for her to come later that morning. She said she wanted to meet the children, then have a private conversation with Martin.

She arrived at about ten. She was a rather small woman with the features that one would expect in a woman named DiMarco. She was probably somewhere in her forties. Her black hair was showing streaks of gray, which she had not attempted to hide. It occurred to Martin that, since he didn't know whether DiMarco was her maiden name or her married name, she was probably of Italian descent either way.

The twins looked apprehensive when they were introduced to her. In their experience, case workers had usually meant a move. They did not relish the prospect of another move now that their lives were showing signs of stability.

Angela DiMarco first asked the children several questions which related to their adjustment. The twins replied positively. It became obvious that they did not want to be moved to another foster home. Martin noticed that they repeatedly referred to him as "Uncle Martin." They were clearly lobbying to stay with him.

After a while, the case worker asked for some privacy with Martin. He suggested that they adjourn to the front porch. The twins seemed somewhat disappointed at being excluded from a conversation which had such a bearing on their future, but they complied with Martin's request that they stay inside. Martin poured lemonade for all of them, then he and Angela DiMarco moved to the front porch.

Her first words were comforting to Martin. "You seem to be getting along quite well. I didn't know what to expect. I read their case file from Chicago, and it sounded like a recipe for disaster."

Martin replied, "I thought so too at first. But fortunately a neighbor woman, a retired school teacher, filled in for their mother's neglect and developed these kids' natural abilities. I was expecting two hellions, but instead I met two underprivileged youngsters who seem to have all the potential in the world. Beyond that, I've become very fond of them, and I'd like to be appointed their legal guardian. I'm willing to be in this for the long haul."

The case worker smiled. "I'll help you with that. It shouldn't be a problem. You know, I work with a lot of throw-away kids whom nobody would want. It's a pleasant surprise to find someone who actually wants any of them."

Martin shook his head. "My wife would have given anything to have a child, but she couldn't. It seems grossly unfair to see women who can give birth annually, but have no maternal instinct. Eloise would have welcomed these kids with open arms."

Angela replied, "I'm really sorry that she didn't live to meet them. But I'll do whatever I can to help you make this work."

Martin said, "I'd really appreciate that. I've arranged piano lessons for them, but soon we'll have to think about school. They've never gone to school, and so I'm concerned about their placement. Their informal education has been rather eclectic. They have learned a lot of things, but I see gaping holes. Beyond that, they have no experience in relating to other kids their age. Even here, there aren't any children close to their age. It's mostly an older neighborhood."

"I can help you with their placement," she said. "I'll arrange to have them tested. We sometimes have that problem with home-schooled children. The standards vary a lot."

Martin sighed. "I feel much better. Since I never had children of my own, I'm really out of it. There's so much about this that I don't know."

Angela smiled again. "I think you're doing just fine. You care a lot. I don't always see that in my work. Please feel free to call me if you have any problems that you can't handle."

With that she left. Martin went inside and was confronted by two worried expressions. He responded with, "She says we're doing just fine. I've asked to become your legal guardian."

Even if the two didn't know exactly what that meant, they caught the implication. They rushed to give him big hugs.

⁂

That evening Martin asked to see the twins' photo album. While Max went to get it, Martin brought out his own album. The children's album was rather small and contained only pictures of them. Jewel was not in any of them, obviously because she had been the photographer.

But none of the photos appeared to have been taken within the last two years.

"How would you like to see some pictures of your mother when she was a little girl?" he asked.

Their response was less enthusiastic than he would have expected, but he opened his album to show the collection of photos which his brother and sister-in-law had sent over the years. The young Jewel appeared to be a normal, happy child.

"Did your mother ever talk to you about her childhood?" he asked.

"Not much," Minnie replied. "She just said that it was unpleasant, and she didn't want to talk about it."

Martin just shook his head. He couldn't imagine what had happened to turn the happy-looking child in the pictures into a woman serving time in prison. However, he sensed that further questions would be unwelcome, and so he just let it pass for the time being.

7

The following Wednesday Martin drove the
twins to Belle Hoskins' house. It was not far
from theirs, but too far to walk. She lived in
a house similar to Martin's with her husband,
who was a high school math teacher, and a fourteen-year-
old son. She greeted them at the door and invited them
in. She had a grand piano in the front room and an old
spinet in a converted bedroom, where she gave lessons.
She obviously wasn't anxious to have beginners banging
on her grand. Martin learned that she didn't have a full-
time job, but supplemented the family income by playing
the organ at the church, accompanying the services at
weddings and funerals, and giving a few private lessons.
That left her ample time to practice.

"I've contacted the piano tuner," said Martin. "He's
coming next week. I don't think it's too badly out of tune,
though. It's a rugged old upright."

"Then it should do for now," replied Belle. "Our first

session will be mainly diagnostic. I'll need to know how far they've progressed before I can place them. I have a lot of used exercise books and sheet music, so you shouldn't have to buy any right away."

"That's fine," said Martin. "I should probably go away while you're working with them. How much time will you need?"

"About an hour and a half. Normally the lessons are just half an hour, but this one will take a little longer."

"Then I'll see you shortly," said Martin and left to take care of some errands.

When he returned, Belle had nearly finished with Max. She was all smiles when she came out and had no problem speaking in front of the children.

"They have had some excellent instruction," she said. "They know nearly everything about reading musical notation. I've never seen that in such young children. They have a good sense of rhythm and dynamics. Beyond that, they seem highly motivated. I don't think you'll have any problem getting them to practice. Frankly, I'm excited about the prospect of working with them."

"That's great news," Martin replied. "I'm really glad that we found you. This is all new to me."

With that, they collected the practice material and departed. As they drove away, Martin asked, "How would you like to go to Baskin-Robbins for some ice cream?"

He didn't have to ask twice.

✦

Two days later Angela DiMarco called to say that she had arranged for the children to take placement tests for school. She gave Martin the time and location for the testing process.

At the appointed time, Martin took the children to an elementary school across town and registered them for the tests. They seemed a little apprehensive at being left at this unfamiliar place, but he assured them that he would be back to pick them up by the time they were finished.

With four hours to kill, Martin went back home and attended to some of his neglected correspondence and bill paying. At the designated time, he drove back to the school and picked up the twins. They looked somewhat stressed from the unaccustomed lengthy testing process. Martin had no idea what the results would be.

He didn't have long to wait. The tests were machine-graded, and so the results were available the same day. Late that afternoon he received a call from Angela DiMarco.

"I need to talk to you," she said. "You have some unusual decisions to make, and it would be better if we could talk in private, and the sooner the better. School starts in September."

"Now I'm intrigued," he said. "My schedule is open. Tell me where and when."

"The children shouldn't hear this yet. Can you be at Luigi's bar and grill at seven?"

Martin smiled as he contemplated the Italian connection.

"OK. I'll meet you there," he said.

﹢〜﹢

After Martin had fed the children and left them to watch TV, he told them that he had to go out for a little while. Having been left alone many times, they just nodded.

Martin drove to the appointed establishment, parked the Buick, and went inside. He found Angela nursing a glass of red wine.

"I suppose you've already eaten," she said.

"Yes. Have you?" he replied.

"No. I'll order something, and you can do as you like."

"I'll just have a glass of wine," he said.

After she had ordered a pasta dish, Angela opened a folder.

"Here are the results of the tests," she said. "Since the twins are nine and have never been to school, we wanted to find out if they could keep up in the fourth grade."

She took a sip of her wine.

"But here is how they placed. According to these, they both scored at the eighth and ninth-grade level on all portions of the tests."

She waited for Martin to absorb the information, then continued. "Now we can't place two nine-year-olds in junior high, and they'd be bored stiff in the fourth grade, and so the question is: Where do we place them?"

Martin pondered the question, then answered, "I'm more concerned with their social development than the academic side. They've never been around other children. But there are also some big gaps in their education. They may be far advanced for their age in math, but I had to teach them how to make change for a dollar. They had never dealt with money."

Angela said, "They obviously have genius IQs, but that is just a measure of potential. Without some educational input, it goes nowhere. Their neighbor teacher in Chicago must have provided that."

"We owe that lady a lot. She seems to have made a retirement project out of Max and Minnie. I should check up on her. But I'm not even sure how to find her."

"I have resources for locating people," said Angela. "But meanwhile we need to decide where to enroll the twins. I have a suggestion."

"I can use one," Martin replied.

"As I see it, any placement in the public school system would be a mismatch. They're too advanced for grade school and too young for junior high or middle school. But there's a special school for gifted children called Halley's. I'd recommend placing them there in the fifth grade. However, there's a catch. It's private, and you'd have to pay for their tuition."

Martin took a long sip on his drink as he mulled over his options. Finally he said, "I didn't bargain for this, but I may have a solution."

"What would that be?" she asked.

"I had a brother, Winston, who was eleven years older than I. He and his wife were Jewel's parents, the twins' grandparents. They both died in a highway accident about ten years ago. Since I was their only known living relative, they had named me as executor in their will. I had to use some vacation time to drive down to Kansas City with Eloise and start to settle their estate. I put their house up for sale through a realtor and sorted through their belongings. I just kept out a few personal items, such as photo albums and family heirlooms, and consigned most of the rest to an auction house. It really felt strange going through someone else's lifetime accumulation."

"I can imagine," she commented.

"I found their will with their personal documents. They had designated twenty percent of their cash assets to me, but the remaining eighty percent was still assigned to Jewel. She had been missing for four years by then, but they had never given up hope for her. That left me with the dilemma of what to do with her share of the estate, since we didn't even know if she was still alive. I consulted the attorney who handled the probate, and he read the fine print of the will. It specified that Eloise was to inherit my share if I died before they did, and Jewel's future 'issue' would claim hers in the same situation. Since Jewel was still missing and I had no knowledge of any 'issue,' I set up a joint savings account in Jewel's and my names. There is a substantial amount sitting in the S&L drawing interest, and Jewel knows nothing about it. She didn't even know that her parents had died until recently. So now the question becomes whether I can tap it for some of the children's expenses."

"I think I can help you there, too," said Angela. "We have a law firm on retainer. I can run the will by them if you'll let me borrow it. They'll be able to tell you the legal ramifications involved."

"I would appreciate that," said Martin. "I'm willing to pay the twins' expenses myself if I have to, but it would be nice to get some help."

Angela replied, "I admire both your honesty and your dedication. I can't imagine where the twins would be or what future they would have without your support."

Martin smiled wanly. "I never expected to become a parent when I'm easily old enough to be a grandparent."

By then he had finished his glass of wine, and she had eaten enough of her meal. They paid their checks and went their separate ways.

8

A few days later, Angela called Martin. "I have two items of news for you, and they're both good," she said. "First, the lawyers have cleared the way for you to be named the twins' legal guardian."

"That's great!" Martin exclaimed. "The kids will be glad to hear that. What's the other one?"

"After examining your brother's will and considering the circumstances, they say that you can tap the joint account for the children's expenses. Just keep detailed records in case anyone should ever ask about it."

"That's a relief," Martin replied. "I can handle their food, clothing, and piano lessons, but tuition for a private school would be a bit of a stretch."

"All right," she said. "I'm glad to be the bearer of glad tidings. I'll talk to you again soon."

With summer past the mid-point, Martin tried to find activities for the twins prior to their first experience with the school system. He bought them swimming suits and took them to a local pool. They enjoyed splashing in the water, but had to stay in the shallow water because of their inability to swim. "One more thing they need to learn," Martin mused. He considered buying them bicycles, but concluded that they weren't ready for those yet. "Maybe by Christmas," he thought. He didn't want to rush them. They were just weeks removed from staying in an apartment all day.

Angela's next call was to tell him that she had contacted the Halley School for Gifted Children and initiated enrollment procedures. The decision to place them in the fifth grade was based on several factors, one of which was the size of the class. Currently there were only twelve children in the class. The small size made it more likely that the teacher would have time to deal with problems individually rather than be swamped by a large number of pupils. Another consideration was that the twins would not be noticeably younger and smaller than their classmates. Social adjustment was just as big a concern as the educational aspect.

✢

Angela continued to telephone Martin almost daily to share information, but one day she had a message which she wanted to deliver in person. She came to his house late in the afternoon. It was still very warm, and so he offered her a glass of iced tea as soon as she came in and waited for her to cool off a little before sharing her news.

"We've located Marian Webster," she said. "After her heart attack, her nephew moved her to a care facility in Des Moines so that she could be close to him and his family. I talked to her this morning. She wanted to know all about the twins. She would love to see them again."

Martin turned to the children and said, "Did you hear that? They've found Miss Webster."

The two smiled broadly.

"I'll give you the address and phone number of the care facility," Angela said. "I assume that you'll want to pay her a visit."

The twins nodded, and Martin said, "Of course."

Then, almost as an afterthought, Angela added, "Would it be possible for me to come along? I'd really like to know more about what went on during those years when she was practically their only link to the outside world. You see, I'm working on a research project about neglected children, and this situation is so unique. Besides, I have a personal interest in this. These kids are really something special."

Martin shrugged. "I don't see why not," he said. "We could leave early one morning and return the same day. You and I could be two 'mice in the corner' while she visits with the kids, then ask her a few questions. There are some things I'd like to know about that learning process. It was unconventional, to say the least."

"Good. How would next Saturday work for you? If you

like, I'll call and make arrangements with Miss Webster and the care facility."

Martin turned to the twins again and asked, "How about it? Would you be willing to skip your piano practice next Saturday and go to see Miss Webster?"

The response was overwhelmingly affirmative.

҂ᝈ҂

The next Saturday the three arose early, picked up Angela, and headed across the Missouri River toward Des Moines. The twins were still groggy from the unusually early awakening and soon fell asleep. That gave the two adults an opportunity for private conversation. She asked him about his past, and he gave her a concise summary of his twenty years in the Army, his marriage to Eloise, his job in middle management at Argus Electrical Company, and his brief period of unemployment. Then it was her turn. She decided to match him for brevity of details, but her account was more personal.

"I grew up near Boston. You've probably picked that up from my accent. Our community was largely Italian. Everyone in our neighborhood was Catholic, and they all sent their brightest kids to Boston College. I went there and majored in sociology. I had always wanted to work with underprivileged kids. While in college, I met a classmate who seemed to share my social concerns. He was also Catholic, but he was Irish, and my family was unhappy with me when we announced our engagement. We were married anyway over the objections of our families on both sides. You'd have to have lived there to understand it. It seemed like a good idea for us to move to a neutral area away from home, and so we both accepted social work jobs in Columbus, Ohio. At first everything went well, but it didn't last long. My husband was having trouble with his job, and he resented the fact that I was doing fine with mine. He started drinking too much and became abusive in ways that I'd rather not mention."

Martin was starting to feel uncomfortable with her personal revelations, but he let her continue.

"I had been taking birth control pills because we were not ready to start a family yet. That made it easier for me to consider divorce. But when I went to confession and told the priest about the pills and my contemplation of divorce, he chastised me for avoiding procreation and told me that it was my Christian duty to uphold the sanctity of marriage. I came away with the feeling that my welfare had been totally subordinated to some kind of dogma. It was a turning point in my life. I went ahead with the divorce and, in the process, alienated both my family and my church. Since then, I have just buried myself in my work. I accepted the job in Omaha just because it was farther away from my problems. I've never regretted it, though. I've had a good life here, and I'm devoted to the people I serve. I miss my family, and I miss my church, but I feel that they abandoned me, not the other way around."

Martin exhaled audibly. This was much more information than he had expected, and he felt somewhat uncomfortable with it. Finally he asked, "Why are you telling me all your secrets? You hardly know me."

She shrugged and said, "You just have that aura about you of being a genuinely good person. I've missed some aspects of my Catholic upbringing. Maybe you qualify as a surrogate for my father confessor."

Martin grinned. "So you picked a Presbyterian as your new father confessor."

She pondered that comment for a moment, then said, "No, I just felt that I'd found a sympathetic soul who shares many of my concerns."

Martin responded, "I'm flattered. I also appreciate having an ally in this situation. I've been entrusted with two children who need a lot of attention, and my experience in such matters is nil. If you can help me with this, I'd be happy to lend a sympathetic ear to your problems, whatever they may be."

She smiled and simply said, "Thanks."

By then the children were stirring, and so they changed the topic of conversation.

9

They reached Des Moines well before noon and located the care facility. The two adults had no idea what to expect, but the twins were excited. They found Marian Webster in the day room, where she had been awaiting their arrival. She was a tall, thin woman of about eighty. When the children ran to her, she extended a hand to each, but did not attempt to hug them. That struck Martin as a little odd until he remembered his own grade school education. A series of single women had always been addressed as "Miss" and had refrained from any display of affection toward their pupils. They had all been competent, but detached. That had been part of their training. No matter how much they may have wanted to hug a pupil, they had been trained to keep the relationship professional. Even in retirement, this woman was still "Miss Webster" to the children, and she did not hug them, even though she was clearly delighted to see them.

For about an hour, Martin and Angela sat and listened while the twins told their former mentor what had happened since her heart attack. It became clear that they were thrilled with their change of fortune, but had fond memories of the many hours they had spent in her apartment. She had taught them, read to them, listened to their first attempts to play her piano, fed them, criticized their mistakes, and praised their successful efforts. In short, she had shaped them.

None of the visitors had given any thought to lunch, but at noon Marian Webster told them that she had arranged for them to eat with her in the facility's dining room. She and the children continued their conversation over lunch.

Afterward, seeing that the exchange of conversation was slowing down, Martin asked her to tell them something about her career and what had transpired during the time in which she had been so important to the development of the twins. He made no attempt to exclude them, since so much of the information was relevant to them.

Miss Webster replied to Martin's inquiry, "I grew up in northern Missouri and attended a teacher's college there. I spent my first four years of teaching in a country school, where I taught all eight grades. It was good experience, but it paid so poorly that I had to look for something better. I responded to an ad in the newspaper for a position teaching sixth grade in a less-than-desirable area of Chicago. I got the job, mainly because nobody else wanted it. I moved into an apartment within walking distance of the school. That way I wouldn't need a car. When I moved into that apartment, I never imagined that I would be staying in it for the next forty-eight years. I managed to establish a rapport with a lot of underprivileged kids and felt that I had contributed something to society. I stayed with the school until they forced me to retire at seventy. I considered moving away then, but there was no place for me to go. The neighborhood had deteriorated further over the years, but there was still a grocery store around the corner as well as a few remaining shops. My nephew and his wife visited me occasionally, but I didn't want to impose upon them. I just stayed home, read a lot, listened to the radio, and practiced my piano. I never cared much for television.

"Then one day a young woman with two small children moved into the apartment across the hall from me. She was a single mother who had just been hired to work in a bar down the street. She seemed desperate to find afford-able day care for her kids. Since I had nothing better to do, I agreed to watch them. The woman, whose name was Jewel, did her best to pay me each week, but as time went on, the hours grew longer and the payments less frequent. I didn't care because I had my retirement check plus social security. What happened was that I became intrigued with those children. They were anything but what one might expect from a single mother who worked in a bar. They were a teacher's dream! They soaked up knowledge like two sponges. They paid attention to everything I said. They even wanted to learn to play my piano. In short, they gave me a reason to continue living.

"When I had my heart attack, the twins were there.

One of them dialed 911. I probably wouldn't be here today if it hadn't been for them."

"Maybe they just returned the favor," said Martin. "If it hadn't been for you, I shudder to think how different they would be today. They have a bright future, and it would hardly have been possible without your enormous contribution."

The woman was clearly touched, but she didn't know what to say.

Martin continued, "We're only a few hours away. We'd like to come back to see you, maybe over Christmas break. Meanwhile, we'll stay in touch."

As they prepared to leave, Minnie rejected her mentor's outstretched hand and asked, "May we kiss you good-bye?"

Miss Webster sat down as the twins each kissed her on the cheek for the first time. She struggled to maintain her composure as they left.

But a subsequent visit was not to be. Two weeks later Martin received notification that a second heart attack had taken the life of Marian Webster. The message came too late for them to attend her funeral. The twins were saddened when they received the news, but as usual, they kept their emotions in check and did not cry.

10

The reported death of Marian Webster reminded Martin that he had heard nothing from Jewel. She surely would want to know what had become of the woman who had played such a significant role in her children's lives. Or maybe not. She had reportedly not been very upset to learn that her own parents had died. But at a minimum, Jewel would want to know how the twins were faring. Martin made a series of phone calls and eventually reached someone in the Illinois Department of Corrections who was able to give him an address for Jewel. Then he sat down and wrote a letter to his prodigal niece, in which he told her of Marian Webster's death and the general details of his assumption of responsibility for her children. He included his telephone number in case she might want to call him.

A few days later he received a late phone call from her.

"Hello, Uncle Martin, this is Jewel," she said.

Martin did not recognize her voice at all, but he had

no reason to doubt that it was his niece. He searched for something to say to her, even though the call was not totally unexpected.

"I was hoping you would call," was the best he could do on the spur of the moment.

"They told me that you have Opal and Onyx," she said.

Martin recalled that those were the twins' names on their birth certificates, but he was somewhat surprised to hear her use them anyway.

"Yes. They'll be starting school next week. They're doing fine," he said.

After a pause, she said, "I'm really glad that you're taking care of them." Another pause. "I suppose you think I'm a terrible mother."

"It's not my place to judge you," Martin replied. "I have no idea what happened to you after you left your parents' home."

"It wasn't pretty," she said. "I made some big-time mistakes, and now I'm paying the price."

"How long do you have to serve?" Martin asked.

"I was sentenced to four years, but it might be reduced if I behave myself," she replied.

"What do they have you doing there?" Martin asked.

"After I finished the de-tox treatment, I actually went back to school. They have a set-up here where us high school drop-outs can get our GED. It's part of their rehab program."

"That sounds good," he said, for lack of a more intelligent reply. "Maybe you'll be able to get a better job after you get out."

"That wouldn't take much," she said. "By the way, are the kids still up?"

"No, they go to bed at nine. They're asleep now."

"Well, give them hugs for me. I'll try to call earlier next time. We don't get much of a choice as to when we can call, though."

"Jewel, would you like for me to bring them to visit you?" he asked.

"Naw," she replied. "I don't want them to see me here. I'll catch up with them after I get out of this place."

"Fine. I'll tell them that for you."

"Well, my time is up," she said. "Somebody else wants to use the phone."

"All right. I'll talk to you again soon. Bye."

After he had hung up, it occurred to Martin that Jewel had never mentioned Marian Webster.

With the beginning of school fast approaching, the need for appropriate clothing was obvious. Once again Alice Flannigan offered to help outfit Minnie, and she met them at Penney's. She and Minnie headed for the girls' department while Martin and Max went the other way. About an hour later they met at the designated counter. When Martin compared their purchases, he wondered why they had bothered to go to separate departments. School clothing for young children had become remarkably unisex. Girls seldom wore skirts or dresses anymore. The winter coats were somewhat more gender-specific, though. With the addition of stocking caps, mittens, and winter boots, the total cost was considerable. Martin decided right away to let his joint account with Jewel cover most of it. It was still too early for lunch, and so Alice left them to do some of her own shopping while Martin and the twins returned home to arrange their new purchases.

Angela stopped by that evening, and the children were eager to show her their clothes. Although there was nothing remarkable about their new wardrobes, it was obviously a big deal for two kids who had never owned new clothes until recently. But Angela had brought two more items. She presented each of them with a red cap with white letters which read: GO BIG RED! The two thanked her politely, but they were clearly mystified.

Angela explained, "Now that you're in Nebraska, you'll have to become Cornhusker fans."

More blank looks.

Angela continued, "With football season approaching, you'll hear a lot about Big Red and the Cornhuskers. The University of Nebraska at Lincoln has a big athletic program. Their football team has won national championships, and a lot of people here are enthusiastic supporters. The University has a smaller branch in Omaha, but its athletic programs are also smaller."

Martin interjected, "They haven't had much exposure to sports. About all we can hope for here is that they'll have some idea what people are talking about and why they're so carried away with it."

"That sounds reasonable," said Angela. "But now, if I may change the subject, I know that you have a parent-teacher conference at the children's school tomorrow. How would it be if I come here and listen to their piano practice, then take them out to lunch?"

Martin turned to the twins and asked, "How does that sound to you?"

As usual, the two looked at each other before responding. Then Max said, "It sounds good to us."

As Angela was leaving, Martin said to her, "They're old enough to be left alone without much concern, but I try to minimize it. They've been left alone too much already. I appreciate your help."

She smiled and said, "You've probably guessed that I have no more official capacity in this since you've become their legal guardian. I just find the situation so intriguing. I want to see how it all turns out."

Martin was stumped for an appropriate reply, but said simply, "You're welcome here any time."

11

The Halley School for Gifted Children was housed in a renovated parochial school, the former occupants of which had moved to a larger facility. Martin drove there the next morning with only the vaguest idea of what to expect. Angela had taken care of the enrollment procedures, and so he was there just for an orientation and a brief meeting with the twins' teacher. The principal of the school, Mr. Sterling, conducted most of the orientation, during which Martin felt somewhat uncomfortable because most of the other people there were at least twenty years younger than he. However, he was relieved to learn that the school had a bus service. Since only a few of the other pupils lived in his area, a small bus would transport the twins along with some children in the lower grades. Martin would not have to drive the twins to and from school. That would enable him to resume his volunteer effort with Meals on Wheels.

Eventually his turn came to meet the children's

teacher. She was a rather short, heavy-set woman of about forty who was introduced to him as Mrs. Wilson. Martin felt relieved that Angela had already submitted a sketchy summary of the twins' background, but Mrs. Wilson still seemed somewhat uncomfortable when she met Martin.

"I'll have to confess that I find your situation unusual," she said. "Most of our pupils come from affluent homes in the suburbs. I don't think we've ever had one whose mother was in prison."

Martin winced at the remark, but tried to maintain his composure.

"I think you'll find the children more compliant than you might expect," he said. "I'm sure that you will agree that it would be detrimental to their welfare if their history were to become common knowledge. Their mother is not in the picture at the moment."

"Of course," she replied. "It would be both professionally and ethically irresponsible for me to divulge personal information. Actually, I'm more curious as to how two children in their situation managed to score so high on the diagnostic tests."

Martin tried to summarize the home-schooling arrangement with Marian Webster as best he could. Then he said, "These are two exceptionally bright youngsters who have had very little exposure to the world outside their apartment building in Chicago. Frankly, I'm more concerned about their social adjustment than any academic issues."

Mrs. Wilson frowned and said, "You must realize that all of the other twelve children in the class have been here for at least two years. I'm not sure how they will respond to two nine-year-olds from Chicago."

Martin shrugged and said, "It will be up to my two to try to fit in. I'll do my best to prepare them."

The teacher tried to appear positive, although she clearly had reservations.

"I'll call you regularly during the first few days and try to give you my perspective on their progress," she said.

"I'd appreciate that," Martin replied.

"I do have one question for you, though," she added. "Do you think I should try to separate them or let them sit together?"

"I'd let them stay together at first," Martin responded. "They've seldom been separated in their young lives." He decided not to add that they even slept and bathed together.

"Fine," she said. "We'll just see what happens. It should be interesting."

"I'm holding my breath and hoping for the best," was his final comment.

Angela and the twins were already back by the time Martin returned.

"Did you three behave yourselves while I was gone?" Martin asked with a grin.

All three smiled back at him, and Minnie answered, "We had fish and chips for lunch."

"What, no spaghetti?" Martin teased.

Angela frowned and said, "Just because I'm Italian doesn't mean that I live on pasta."

Martin grinned and changed the subject for lack of a quick response.

"I met Mrs. Wilson today," he said. "She'll be their teacher. She's aware of the general situation and seems to have a handle on it."

"That's good," said Angela. "I think that our new pupils are ready for her."

"I'm ready to go to a real school," said Minnie. "It will be kind of an adventure."

Max just shrugged and said, "I have no idea what to expect. We've never gone to a real school."

Angela tried to remain positive. "I think you'll be just fine," she said. "You'll make some friends and have a good experience."

The twins' expressions betrayed some doubt, but they didn't say anything.

Martin sensed that the conversation had run its course and invited Angela to stay for supper.

"Thanks," she said, "but I have some more work to do. I should keep moving."

After some prompting from their uncle, the twins thanked her for the lunch, and she left.

꠸꠵꠸

Later that evening the telephone rang, and Martin answered it. It was an Illinois operator asking if he would accept collect charges from Jewel. Martin said that he would, and Jewel spoke.

"I only have a few minutes," she said. "Can I talk to the kids?"

Martin called the twins, and each spoke to Jewel for a minute or two. He noticed that neither of them showed much emotion or interest in talking to their mother. Max handed the phone back to Martin after having told Jewel that he was looking forward to school.

Jewel's next request came as no surprise. She wanted to know if Martin could send her a few dollars. He promised to do so. Then, against his better judgment, Martin told her about her parents' estate and that he was using part of it to cover her children's expenses. He tried to assure her that there would be a significant amount left to help her get established after her prison stay was over. She wanted to know how much there was, but Martin honestly told her that he didn't know. He immediately sensed that he had already told her too much, but he had already let the proverbial cat out of the bag.

12

The twins' first day of school was preceded by the kind of anxiety which was usually typical of kindergartners. It was with mixed feelings that Martin watched them board the mini-bus for their first day of school as fifth graders. After tending to some household chores, he left to deliver his Meals on Wheels. He had a Monday-Wednesday-Friday route with just six deliveries. He was back home again by early afternoon. Although he tried to stay busy, his mind was on the children and their adjustment to what for them was a strange environment.

The telephone rang at shortly after three. It was Mrs. Wilson.

"I thought you might like to hear how the children's first day of school went," she said.

"Certainly," Martin replied.

"Since there obviously has been no preparation from them by then, I usually ask the children to tell how they spent the summer. Most of them had taken a trip of some kind. Your two explained that they had just moved here from Chicago and hadn't gone anywhere else. But then they went on to describe their fascination with some rather ordinary sights and events around here. Since I knew a little about their background, I could understand that, but the other children seemed to think it a little odd."

"I can imagine," said Martin.

"Later I heard a girl tell Minnie that she had been to Chicago and had visited the Museum of Science and Industry and taken the elevator to the top of Sears Tower. Minnie seemed embarrassed to admit that she had never been to either."

"Well, I suppose that's to be expected," Martin replied. "But other than that, how did they get along?"

"They seemed reluctant to volunteer anything, but when I called on them, they responded well. My sense is that they will adjust to the routine, but it will take some time."

"Since they're only nine, they have plenty of that," he said.

"Meanwhile, I'll keep you informed," she said.

"That will help me a lot," was Martin's final comment.

❦

When the twins returned home, they seemed eager to tell Martin about their first day of school. One of the first items was that they would need a few more school supplies than just the pens, pencils, tablets, and rulers which they already had. Martin duly noted the required items and promised to pick them up the next day. Then the two children described their first day in a real school after their lengthy tutorial.

"Mrs. Wilson told us that no pocket calculators would be allowed in math class. We were the only ones who didn't look disappointed. We've never used a pocket calculator."

Martin felt an urge to tell them that he had carried a slide rule to math class in high school, but thought better of it. Few children would have any idea what a slide rule was.

Martin felt relieved when the two children went to practice their piano lessons. Nothing catastrophic had happened during their first day of school, and they appeared positive about their situation.

Mrs. Wilson called twice more that week, but had no startling news. That Friday afternoon Angela showed up for a visit. This time she was able to stay for supper. Martin grilled hot dogs and had made potato salad. The twins had already practiced their piano lessons, but they played for Angela at her request. They played a duet that Mozart had written to perform with his sister when they were both children. Martin couldn't help but think how much Eloise would have enjoyed having so much music in the house.

After the impromptu concert, Angela asked the children to report on their first days of school. Minnie responded first.

"In the morning we have English, math, and social studies. Mrs. Wilson teaches those. Then we have fifteen minutes of aerobic exercises before lunch. Everyone in the school meets in the gym for that. Then we have a light lunch in the cafeteria. They seem determined to keep us from gaining too much weight. It's not bad, though. After lunch we have different subjects on different days. We have music three days a week and art the other two. Sometimes we have science class, and sometimes we have computer lab. We haven't been there long enough to know the exact schedule, though. Some time each afternoon we have a study hall. They try to give us time to do most of our homework there so we can get extra help if we need it. We haven't needed any help yet, though."

Angela nodded approvingly, then asked, "How are you getting along with your classmates?"

There was a pause before either replied, but eventually Max said, "We don't fit in very well. They talk to each other about their computer games, down-loading music on their iPods, and their favorite rock groups. We don't even know what they're talking about, and they seem to find us kinda weird."

"Well, you're not weird," Angela defended. "You just came from a different situation. If you think that computer games and text-messaging are important, we can do something about that."

Minnie replied, "Actually we don't care about those things. We have more than we'd ever dreamed of, and we're really happy. Our world is so much bigger than it was. If the other kids think we're odd, we can live with that. Sometimes we think that they're the ones who are odd."

Angela looked pensive for a moment, then said, "I wonder how many of your classmates know about your piano playing."

The twins just shrugged.

"I'll bet your music teacher would let you play that Mozart duet at the beginning of class. It would only take a few minutes. Why don't you ask her?"

Minnie looked skeptical. "The music they like doesn't sound anything like Mozart," she said.

"Maybe you can teach them something," said Angela. "It would be worth a try."

Max replied, "OK. I'll ask her next time. We have music class with the sixth graders."

Having agreed on a plan of action, they switched to other topics.

❧

The next Monday, Mrs. Wilson phoned before the twins returned home from school.

"Your two certainly got some attention today," she said. "They played a duet for their music class that just stunned the other kids. The music teacher was so impressed that she called the principal, Mr. Sterling, and me to come and hear a repeat performance. All of a sudden your two outsiders became minor celebrities. Mr. Sterling asked them to play for the next PTA meeting. I'm no musician, but I know talent when I hear it, and your twins have it."

Martin smiled and said, "I just hope that this translates into some measure of social acceptance. That has been slow in coming."

"I'm sure it will," the teacher replied. "You should have seen the expressions on the other children's faces when the twins started to play. They didn't need a music appreciation course to tell them that this was something special."

Shortly after they had concluded their conversation, the twins arrived home. They were all excited about the results of their performance.

"Just wait until we tell Miss DiMarco!" Max exclaimed.

13

The rest of September was marked with advancement in nearly all areas of the twins' development. They made steady progress with their piano lessons, and Belle Hoskins even started instructing them on the organ after church. Martin introduced them to the youth group at church with the dual purpose of broadening their social circle and exposing them to religious education. On Saturday afternoons they donned their GO BIG RED caps and watched the Cornhusker football team on television. Gradually they learned the rules of the game, even if they had some reservations about the violence of it. Neither of them showed much inclination toward athletics, but Martin bought a softball and taught them to play catch with it.

Even though the curriculum of the school was enriched in order to challenge exceptionally bright children, Max and Minnie had no trouble keeping up. Martin was relieved to find that he would seldom be asked to help them with their homework, and he offered a silent thank-you to the ghost of Marian Webster. She had not only taught them well, but she had also encouraged them to think for themselves. Consequently, their analytical skills were excellent. Mrs. Wilson stopped calling Martin after the twins had gained a measure of social acceptance.

Angela DiMarco continued to drop by and maintain contact. The twins were always glad to see her, and Martin welcomed a female presence in the house, since he was trying to be both father and mother to the children in the absence of both.

Another sign of adjustment was that Minnie was sleeping in her own bed, possibly preferring the less crowded situation. Martin hoped that they would also learn some degree of modesty before reaching puberty, but he was reluctant to make an issue of it. He speculated that their mother had been rather liberal in that regard.

⁀✢⁀

One morning, as the twins were boarding their mini-bus for school, Martin noticed a man sitting in his car across the street watching them. After the bus left, the man got out of his car and approached Martin's house. He was a casually dressed man of about thirty-five. He seemed rather nervous as he approached. Martin met him at the front door.

"I need to talk to you," the man said without preamble.

"About what?" Martin asked.

"I'm Opal and Onyx's father," he replied.

Somewhat against his better judgment, Martin invited the man inside. Both sat down in the living room. Martin looked at the younger man and waited for him to initiate the conversation.

"My name isn't important," he said. "I lived with Jewel in Chicago after she ran away from home. I wanted to marry her, but she was still under-aged and couldn't very well ask for her parents' permission. We were together on and off over the years, and I just found out that she was in prison."

"So you knew about the children," Martin said.

"Yeah, but I wasn't in any position to support a family."

"Are you now?" Martin asked.

"Not really," the man replied. "That's why I'm here to offer you a deal."

"And just what would that be?" Martin asked as he tried to contain and conceal his disgust.

"I figure I could claim parental rights to the kids if I wanted to. But they're better off with you. Jewel told me about the money her parents left her, and that you hold the purse strings. I figure it would be a better deal for you to give me half of the money and I would sign away any rights to the kids."

Martin struggled to retain his composure. Finally he said, "I'd have to look into it. I'm not even sure how much is there."

"Hey, it has to be six figures, doesn't it?"

"Possibly. I'd have to check on it as well as what kind of agreement you'd have to sign to renounce your claim," Martin replied.

"All right! You do that, and I'll be in touch," the man said.

"Maybe by then you'll even have a name," Martin countered sarcastically.

"It's Jasper," the man said.

With that, the man offered his hand. Martin ignored it, turned, and walked away, leaving his uninvited guest to find his own way out.

After the man had gone, Martin dialed Angela's cell phone number. When she answered, he said, "Houston, we have a problem."

14

ngela came to Martin's house as soon as she could get away, and he gave her a detailed account of his unexpected visit.

"I think I should have a nice long talk with my niece," he said. "She must have told him about her parents' estate. There's no other way he could have found out about it. But it doesn't sound as if she's included in his scheme."

"That would be a good idea," she replied. "But you'd have to go to her in order to have much of a conversation. I'd be happy to stay here with the twins while you're gone. But meanwhile we'll have to deal with this Jasper character here. If you like, I'll come here to offer whatever advice I may have for you."

"That would be great," Martin said. "I suspect that he's some kind of a loser who just thinks he's found a big opportunity, but I'd hate to gamble the kids' future on it."

"Just call me on my cell phone when he contacts you

again, and I'll get away. My schedule gives me that kind of flexibility."

"Thanks a lot," he said. "This is too important for me to try to deal with it by myself."

⌁

Martin didn't have to wait long for his next contact. The phone rang the next morning right after the twins had left for school. Martin guessed that Jasper was sitting in his car holding a cell phone, but he had no way of knowing. As soon as he had agreed to meet with Jasper, he called Angela. She rushed right over and narrowly beat Jasper there.

When Jasper saw Angela, he looked even more uncomfortable than usual. "Who is this?" he asked Martin.

"This is Miss DiMarco," Martin replied. "She's the twins' case worker. I want to get her advice on this matter."

Jasper obviously hadn't counted on having an outsider there.

"What's there to discuss?" he asked. "I'm offering you my rights as a parent in exchange for half of an estate which should be mine anyway."

Angela spoke for the first time. "Maybe we should hear just what your relationship was with Jewel and the children. Why don't you start from the beginning?"

Jasper fidgeted as he tried to collect his thoughts. "I started seeing Jewel in Kansas City when she was fifteen. When her parents found out about it, they tried to keep us apart. I was six years older than her. Finally, Jewel got tired of their meddling in her personal life and agreed to run away to Chicago with me."

So far, his story seemed plausible, Martin thought.

"When we got to Chicago, we stayed with some of my buddies until we could get jobs and rent an apartment. Jewel worked in a motel as a maid for a while, then got a job as a waitress at a truck stop. She'd never had a social security card before, so nobody could trace her from that. I went through several jobs, but none of them worked out for me. I was drawing unemployment when she got pregnant. I wanted to take her to an abortion clinic, but she didn't want to go. When she gave birth to twins, I freaked out. I told her I'd leave her if she didn't give them up for adoption. She told me to go ahead, so I did. After that we had an on-and-off relationship until she took a job as a waitress in a bar somewhere. I didn't see her again until somebody told me she was in prison. I still cared about her, so I went there to see her last month."

"Gee, that was decent of you," said Angela. "She must have been thrilled to see you after all that time."

Jasper ignored the sarcasm and said, "Actually she was. Nobody else seemed to care about her."

"So she told you that her parents had died and left her most of their estate," said Martin.

"Right. And she told me about her Uncle Martin in Omaha, who hadn't bothered to go to see his niece in prison."

Martin decided not to be intimidated into making a defensive comment. Instead, he took an offensive approach.

"Just what makes you think that you're entitled to part of her estate?" he asked.

Jasper replied, "She was my common-law wife and gave birth to my children."

"And just how much have you contributed to the support of those children?" Angela asked.

"Hey, I didn't even know where they were most of the time," he replied.

"Still, you could be held liable for nine years of back child support," said Angela. "That could put quite a dent in your fortune."

Jasper sputtered as he tried unsuccessfully to form a response.

"I have a different concern," said Martin. "I see that you have blue eyes. Jewel also has blue eyes. Minnie—Opal—has brown eyes. Do you know that it is impossible for two blue-eyed parents to produce a brown-eyed child?"

Jasper's mouth fell open. "Do you mean she was cheating on me?" he asked.

"Heavens! How could any woman do that to a man like you?" asked Angela. "But of course this puts a big damper on your claim. A DNA test would prove that you are not the twins' father."

Jasper was speechless as he saw his plot crumbling.

Martin used the lapse to conclude, "I think your claim just evaporated. So why don't you just leave before I call the police and have you arrested for fraud?"

Jasper heeded Martin's advice and beat a hasty retreat. Martin and Angela watched him head for his car and waved him a symbolic good-bye.

Martin spoke first after the man had left. "Thanks for your support. I don't know how it would have gone if you hadn't been here to back me up."

Angela smiled. "I'm really glad I was able to help," she said. "But I do have one question for you. Are you sure about that blue-eyed, brown-eyed bit?"

Martin grinned back at her. "I have no idea. It's just something I read somewhere."

15

Martin waited until his next collect call from Jewel to schedule a trip to Illinois to talk to her. He told her about the visit from Jasper and said that he wanted to discuss it in more detail than a phone call would allow. It came as no big surprise that "Jasper" was actually a Walter.

After coordinating arrangements with Angela, he made plans for a two-day trip to Illinois. The prison was a minimum-security women's facility near Peoria. It was just far enough away that he didn't care to try for a one-day trip. He had no idea how long it would take him to conclude his business with Jewel.

On a pleasant October day, Martin made the drive across Iowa and reached the correctional facility by mid-afternoon. It just took a short time for him to check in and meet his niece in a private room. There was no glass partition as portrayed in the movies. Martin was startled by Jewel's appearance, but he tried not to let it show.

She looked several years older than she was. He would not have recognized her as the pretty child in the photograph album. She looked at him expressionlessly, thereby removing any notion on his part of attempting to hug her. She sat down opposite him at a table and seemed prepared for some kind of an ordeal.

"Would you like to see some recent pictures of the children?" he asked, trying to break the ice.

Her expression softened immediately. "Of course," she replied.

Martin took out a photo envelope and handed it to her. She ignored him while she looked at the pictures. Finally she remarked, "They've grown. They've also gained some weight."

Martin just nodded and resisted an impulse to say that eating regularly would have that effect.

"May I keep these?" Jewel asked.

"Certainly. I can always take more," he said.

Jewel put the photos back into the envelope and held them in front of her on the table, as if she were afraid that someone might take them away from her.

Then she said, "It's been a long time, Uncle Martin. I hardly remembered what you looked like."

He nodded. "That goes both ways. You were only about twelve or thirteen the last time I saw you."

She lowered her gaze and said, "A lot has happened since then. Not much of it very good."

"So I've gathered," Martin replied. "I'd be interested in hearing your side of what happened."

Jewel took a deep breath and began. "I was fifteen

when I met Walter. He was twenty-one and treated me like an adult. I was flattered by the attention of a grown man with a car who made me feel like somebody special. My parents treated me like the teen-ager I was. I rebelled against them when they told me to stop seeing Walter. He said he loved me and wanted to be with me always. I was too young and stupid to realize that he was a loser who couldn't have attracted a woman his own age. When he asked me to run away to Chicago with him, I said yes. It didn't even occur to me to think about what it would do to my parents.

"When we got to Chicago, we stayed with his cousin while we both looked for jobs. I could always get a min-imum-wage job, but Walter kept looking for something that paid a lot without requiring much effort. So he was drawing unemployment most of the time while I was making enough to keep us from starving. But I was still in love with him and bought his excuses. He said he wanted to marry me, but we'd have to wait until I was old enough to get a license without my parents' consent. By the time I was old enough, I had wised up enough to realize what a jerk he was. But whenever I'd talk about going back home, he'd feed me another line about how it would all change. He'd go away for days at a time, supposedly to look for a better-paying job, but he'd always come back. Once he was gone for over a month, and I made the big-gest mistake yet. I was working at a truck stop café when one of the other waitresses invited me to go with her to a party downtown. She said that some college guys were graduating, and their parents were throwing a big bash for them. There would be lots of fancy food and plenty of free drinks. It sounded like fun, and so I went along. It *was* a lot of fun. I met some classy people and pretended to be one of them. The food and the drinks were just there for the taking. I was having a good time and didn't worry about anything."

Jewel suddenly looked somber.

"The next morning I woke up in a motel bed with my clothes on the floor and a fifty-dollar bill on the table. I couldn't remember anything after feeling a little dizzy at the party. My head hurt, and my tongue felt like the Russian army had walked over it barefoot. I took a shower and called a cab. At least they had left me cab fare. But I soon found out that they had left me more than that. I was pregnant.

"When Walter returned, I didn't know I was pregnant yet, and we continued our on-again, off-again relationship. When he found out that I was expecting, he assumed that it was his and predictably freaked out. He wanted me to have an abortion, but something from my neglected set of ethics said no. Walter responded in his true fashion by leaving again. I didn't see him again for over a year. He always managed to come back when he needed something, even if it was just a meal and a place to sleep. When the time came for the 'blessed event,' I went to the welfare clinic along with the other poor wretches who had no health insurance and no money. I had thought about giving up the baby for adoption, not knowing that there were two, but when I saw those little faces, I knew that I couldn't. I got a room in public housing and lived on public assistance for three or four years. There was a black woman from Tennessee with two babies on my floor. She and I took turns taking care of each other's kids while the other one went out. We both got part-time jobs on different shifts and survived. But eventually she decided to go back to Tennessee. That left me in a big bind. I had to find a job and day care. The twins were out of diapers by then, which was a bigger relief than you can imagine. With no real job skills, the best I could do was to wait tables and pour drinks in a bar in a poor neighborhood. I rented a two-room apartment near the bar and hoped that I could find someone to stay with my kids while I was working. That was when I met Miss Webster, who lived across the hall. She was a godsend."

Martin nodded as he recalled the tall, thin woman who had made such a difference in the twins' lives.

Jewel continued, "But maybe she was a mixed blessing. She was lonely and would take the kids whenever I asked. When I couldn't pay her, she never seemed to mind. So I took advantage of her. She made it possible for me to have a social life as well as hold a full-time job. The kids got so used to having me gone that they didn't seem to notice when I left them alone. I was enjoying the kind of freedom that I had given up when I ran away with Walter. Unfortunately, the crowd I hooked up with was into booze and drugs, and I went along with them. Maybe it was for the best that I got caught dealing and sent here. After Miss Webster had her heart attack, I neglected my kids something awful. It hurt to have them taken away from me, but I can see now that it was better for them.

I'm really grateful to you for taking them in and looking after them. It seems that you and Miss Webster have been their real parents."

Martin was somewhat surprised by her contrition, but he simply shrugged and said, "No problem. They've done nearly as much for me as I have for them. After losing my wife and my job, I was at loose ends."

For the first time, Jewel managed a faint smile. Then she said, "I have no idea where we go from here. I should be out on parole in a few months, but I probably won't be allowed to leave the state. I'll need to find a job and try to get my act together."

Martin offered, "Your parents' estate account will help. It will cover a place to live and a car to drive."

She threw up her hands. "I don't even know how to drive. I was just starting to learn when I left home."

"We'll arrange for some driver training and get you squared away. If you can't leave the state, I'll bring the twins to see you once in a while."

Jewel put her head in her hands. "I don't even know if they'll want to see me. I've messed up so badly. Maybe I should just stay out of their lives. I must be a big embarrassment to them."

Martin replied, "I can't speak for them, but I'll talk to them. So far, they haven't said much about you one way or another."

She shrugged and said, "I guess that's about the best I can hope for. Maybe they won't hate me."

"I don't think that's even in their nature. They're really remarkable kids. You must have done something right."

Jewel looked skeptical and said, "Wouldn't that be the wonder of the ages?"

"Don't be so hard on yourself. You've messed up, but your life isn't beyond repair. Try to focus on the future. You still have a lot of living to do. I'll try to help you, if you'll let me."

She seemed to find the offer ironic. "Just what you need," she said, "one more kid to take care of."

Martin was not amused. He said, "I don't plan to take care of you. I'm just offering to make it easier for you to take care of yourself. I'm the twins' legal guardian and the executor of your parents' estate. That puts me in a position to help you a lot, and I'm ready to do that as long as you do your share. But if you go back to your old habits, you'll be on your own. I won't bail you out of jail or get you into a de-tox program. Do we understand each other?"

She looked startled, but said, "Loud and clear. But don't worry. I know a good deal when I hear it."

"Fine," he said. "I'll be back to see you every so often, and I'll bring more photos. After you're out of here, I'll bring the twins along. By the way, they prefer 'Minnie and Max' to 'Opal and Onyx.' And they're doing really well."

As Martin stood to leave, Jewel surprised him by putting her arms around him and giving him a big hug. He couldn't remember her ever doing that as a child.

"Thank you, Uncle Martin," she said. "You've just given me my life back."

16

After spending a nearly sleepless night in a motel, Martin drove home the next day with mixed feelings about his visit. Jewel had seemed sincere about reforming, but he was wary of accepting her apparent contrition on face value. Time would tell. He'd had little experience with drug addicts. Meanwhile, he was uncertain about what he should tell the twins. He decided to wait and see what they asked. So far they had shown remarkably little interest in their mother and her situation. That seemed to be the primary by-product of her neglect. They didn't hate her or even dislike her. She had simply become a non-factor in their lives.

As he approached Omaha, Martin stopped at a rest stop and tried to call Angela. She didn't answer, and so he just left a message on her answering machine to say that he would be back by the time the children came home from school.

+~+

October passed with no major events. When Martin asked the twins if they would like to go trick-or-treating on Halloween, they declined. They considered themselves too old to participate in that kind of activity.

November brought the usual change in the weather pattern as well as the usual round of germs and viruses. Max caught a cold and soon shared it with his sister. After consulting Alice, Martin kept them home from school for two days, mainly to keep them from spreading their malady any further, but they recovered quickly. They appeared to have good immune systems.

On the seventh Martin quietly and privately observed the anniversary of his wife's passing. He was not inclined to show his emotions under any circumstances, and that trait carried over to this occasion. The twins noticed that he was quieter than usual, but since it hardly affected them, they let it pass without comment. He was glad to be able to spend the day alone with his thoughts and memories. Any visit would have seemed like an intrusion. Still, he was aware that the passage of time was providing a healing effect on his grief. The inclusion of the twins had also helped fill the void in his life.

As Thanksgiving approached, Martin decided to prepare a big traditional feast. On his next trip to the commissary he bought a turkey and most of the accessories. The twins had never experienced a dinner with turkey and all the trimmings, and so he decided to introduce them to the custom. He also invited Angela and the Flannigans to join them for the occasion. When they offered to bring something, he only agreed to let Alice bring a pumpkin pie and Angela a cranberry salad, since he had no experience making either. He considered himself a fairly good cook, but it was within a limited range. He was reluctant to try anything very complicated.

When the big day arrived, Martin arose early and made a light breakfast for himself and the twins.

"You'll want to save your appetites for dinner," he told them. Then he had them set the dining room table while he started the culinary process.

The guests arrived shortly before noon. Angela and the Flannigans had heard so much about each other that introductions hardly seemed necessary.

While Martin put the finishing touches on dinner, the twins played the piano for their guests. Mike Flannigan had never heard them play before and was greatly impressed. He said to Martin, "I was expecting "Twinkle, Twinkle Little Star" and instead I got Chopin. Wow!"

After Martin had started to carve the turkey, they all sat down at the table. Martin said grace, and they proceeded with the meal. There was little conversation while they ate. Each one was too busy enjoying the feast. After their plates were all clean, Martin asked if they were ready for dessert. They all agreed to postpone the pumpkin pie until later, after they had digested some of the main meal. Angela helped the twins clear the table and load the dishwasher, after which they all adjourned to the living room.

At first the Flannigans felt awkward starting an adult conversation with two young children present, but it soon became apparent that the twins could hold their own with adult conversation. They showed no inclination to leave.

Eventually the topic of humor came up when Mike mentioned his favorite sit-com on television. Nobody else had watched it, and so Mike tried to summarize an episode. When nobody reacted, he switched gears and said, "You know, humor is a little like music. It's subjective. Different people have different tastes. But most of us like some kind of music and some kind of humor. We're unique among God's creatures that way. No other animal creates music or has a sense of humor."

"Maybe those are special gifts," said Martin.

Turning to the twins, Mike said, "I can see what kind of music you like. What kind of jokes do you like?"

Max shrugged and said, "We don't know any."

It suddenly occurred to Martin that in the months he had spent with the two, he had never seen them laugh or cry, even when they learned of Miss Webster's death.

Mike continued, "Well, it seems that part of your education has been neglected. We'll have to work on that."

Alice rolled her eyes. "Here we go!" she said. "Mike, try to keep it clean."

Mike grinned and replied, "I do know one or two clean jokes. Here's one: A man is walking down the street when he meets another man who has a banana sticking out of his left ear. The first man says, 'Hey, do you know you have a banana in your ear?' The other man says, 'Huh?' The first man repeats, 'I said, you've got a banana in your ear.' The other man says, 'I can't hear you. I've got a banana in my ear.'"

Martin and Angela chuckled. The twins smiled politely. Alice said, "Mike, that's the dumbest joke I've ever heard."

"OK, Smarty, you try it," said Mike.

Alice thought for a moment, then said, "Here's an old one. A woman goes to the refrigerator and opens the door. Much to her surprise, there's a rabbit sitting in there. She asks it, 'What are you doing in there?' The rabbit shrugs and says, 'Isn't this a Westinghouse?' She says, 'Yes.' The rabbit says, 'I'm just westing.'"

She got a slightly better reaction than Mike had.

"All right, Angela, it's your turn," said Mike.

Angela cringed and said, "I'm not a very good joke teller."

"Like we are?" Alice asked.

After a brief pause, Angela said, "Here's one from my Catholic upbringing. A nun walks into a bar with a parrot on her shoulder. The bartender looks at her and asks, 'Where did you get that?' The parrot answers, 'The Vatican. They've got a lot of them.'"

By then the twins were getting into the spirit of the session and were obviously enjoying it. Minnie said, "It's your turn, Uncle Martin."

Martin shook his head and said, "I haven't told a joke in a long time."

"Well, then, it's about time," said Alice.

Martin reluctantly agreed. He began, "Up in Minnesota there are a lot of Scandinavians, and they tell stories about a not-too-bright couple named Ole and Lena. But, in the spirit of political correctness, some people started worrying about the possibility of offending someone by telling an ethnic joke. So someone got the idea of substituting an extinct civilization for the current ones. Rather than telling Norski, Jewish, or Iowan jokes, we should make them Hittites. Since those people disappeared about three thousand years ago, nobody could be offended. So there were these two Hittites, Ole and Lena--"

The story telling continued for quite a while, with Mike providing most of the jokes. Eventually Alice suggested that their dinner might have settled enough for them to contemplate a slice of pumpkin pie.

"That will take care of supper for me," said Martin. "Does anyone else want a turkey sandwich?"

No one else wanted any more than pie to eat the rest of the day. They were all comfortably full.

Around eight the guests got ready to leave. As was her custom, Alice hugged all the others while the men stood there awkwardly. Then Angela followed her example. It gave Martin a strange feeling to have her hug him. He hadn't been prepared for that.

The next day was a non-school day, but Martin still had to deliver his Meals on Wheels. He took the twins with him while he made his deliveries, but they stayed in the car while he took the food in. On the way home, he explained to them that this was a big shopping day. Many people did their Christmas shopping because the retail stores offered discounts in order to entice them. He also explained that he preferred to do his Christmas shopping when the stores were less crowded. That gave him a good excuse to avoid any further excursions. They went home and ate left-overs from the feast of the previous day.

〜

One day the following week the twins came home from school with the announcement that they had learned a joke, but didn't understand it very well. Minnie explained.

"The kids found out that our real names are Opal and Onyx, and two boys told us this one:

Minnie: Knock, knock!

Max: Who's there?

Minnie: Opal

Max: Opal who?

Minnie: Opal up your pants! I was just kidding."

Martin cringed and tried to think how much he should try to explain. Finally he simply said, "I think you understand enough to realize that it's pretty naughty. I'd suggest that you keep it quiet and don't tell it again."

The twins seemed satisfied with that and went to practice their piano lessons.

17

With Thanksgiving behind them, Martin started thinking about Christmas. He would have to give some thought about what to buy for the twins and how to decorate the house. He also wanted to visit Jewel again shortly before Christmas. He would have to check with Angela to see if she would be available to stay with the children. He didn't know if she had any plans for the holidays. She always seemed to make herself available when he needed help, but he didn't want to take advantage of her.

As usual, the weeks before Christmas passed quickly. Martin bought two small bicycles and an assortment of books and CDs for the twins and stashed them at the Flannigans' house. His Christmas card list had dwindled over the years, especially after Eloise's death. He wrote a form letter to enclose with the cards giving everyone a report on the twins and their progress. It occurred to him that some of them didn't even know about his new family yet. One Saturday Angela helped him and the children decorate the house for Christmas. He hadn't done any decorating the previous three years. "What a difference a year makes," he thought as he looked at the ornaments. For the twins it was a new experience. They had never decorated their apartment or done much of anything else to celebrate the occasion.

About a week before Christmas, Martin made arrangements for the trip to Peoria to visit Jewel. The twins had written letters, and he had taken some new pictures of them. Angela had agreed to spend the night with them while he was away. He would have to buy her a nice present, but he was at a loss as to what to get her. Maybe Alice would have a suggestion, he thought.

The sky was overcast, but the road was dry as Martin made his second trip to Peoria. He had waited until after making his Meals on Wheels delivery, and so it was late afternoon by the time he reached the correction facility. This time Jewel looked somewhat more presentable than she had on his previous visit. She hugged him without saying anything and sat down at the table opposite him. He handed her the envelope containing the letters and photos of the twins. Jewel looked at the pictures immediately, but saved the letters to read later.

"How are you getting along?" he asked.

She shrugged. "It's going. I'm taking a computer class now. They say I'll need to know something about them for just about any kind of work other than making beds and busing tables."

"Any word on when you'll get out of here?" he asked.

"They say maybe as early as next spring. The place is getting to be so crowded that they're trying to get rid of some of us as soon as possible," she replied.

"How about job prospects? Will they help you with placement?"

"Yeah. They have connections with several do-gooder businesses that hire non-violent types. I'm looking for something in accounting. I'm better with numbers than I am with writing. I never learned spelling and grammar very well."

"Maybe we'll get the twins to help you," Martin said. "They're good at it."

She smiled wryly. "Wouldn't that be something? I never taught them much of anything."

"At least you arranged for somebody else to do it. They're doing really well in school. After another year where they are, we'll see about getting them into an honors program at a middle school or a junior high."

They talked for another half hour, then Martin gave her a fifty dollar bill just before leaving.

"Here's a little Christmas present," he said. "I didn't know what else to get you."

"This is more than I could have expected," she said. "I'm sorry I'm not in a position to get you and the kids anything."

"They'll understand," he said. "Maybe next Christmas will be different."

"I'll have to live in a half-way house after I get out of here," she said. "I don't know how long that will be. Meanwhile, I won't be allowed to leave the state."

"We'll just take it as it comes," said Martin. "Meanwhile, you take care of yourself."

She hugged him again as he prepared to leave and thanked him for coming to see her.

✛✛

Just before Christmas, Angela invited Martin and the twins to go with her on a special trip. They stopped at a supermarket and picked up several large bags of groceries. Then they delivered them to needy families in a poorer part of the city. The twins helped carry some of the bags, but didn't say anything until they were finished.

"What did you think of that?" Martin prompted.

Max answered in a soft voice, "Last Christmas somebody left a bag of groceries outside our door."

Martin and Angela looked at each other, but neither of them was able to formulate a response.

✛✛

When Martin told Angela that he was planning to take the twins to a church service Christmas Eve, she surprised him by asking to go along.

"Have you ever attended a Protestant Christmas Eve service?" he asked.

"No," she replied, "but I assume that you celebrate the same birthday as the Catholics."

Martin felt mildly embarrassed, but responded, "When all is said and done, it's remarkable how much antagonism and bitterness there has always been over how to get to heaven."

"I agree," she replied. "But at least we don't kill each other over it anymore."

"Maybe we learned something from the Thirty Years' War."

"Let's hope so. But this is getting pretty heavy," she said. "If it's all right with you, I'd like to watch the children open their presents, too. I'll bring my camera."

"You're always welcome. I take it that you haven't made any other plans for the holidays," he said.

"No, but there's always some kind of a problem that arises among my cases. Some people are depressed at Christmas and cause trouble. I need to be ready to respond."

Martin just shook his head. "That's quite a job you have," he said.

✢✢✢

The Christmas Eve service was well organized. Martin reflected on how much of the religious tradition the children had absorbed in the previous two months. They were familiar with most of the Christmas carols and sang along. Again they were enchanted by Belle Hoskins' organ playing.

After the service, they went back home to continue the celebration. "Santa," a.k.a. Mike Flannigan, had delivered the bicycles and the wrapped presents during their absence. The children were thrilled. It occurred to Martin that, for once, they actually seemed like two nine-year-olds. Since the two had no money to buy presents, they gave Martin and Angela art projects that they had made at school. In addition to presents for the twins, Angela gave Martin a wool sweater. At Alice's recommendation, he had bought her a pretty silk scarf and some of her favorite perfume.

When the time came for her to leave, Angela hugged and kissed each of the children. Then she surprised Martin by kissing him, too. It just seemed natural to her, but it was unexpected for him nonetheless. The twins showed no reaction to it at all. For the first time, Martin sensed that Angela's attention was not entirely focused on the children.

18

Mid-winter was unusually mild, and the twins were able to begin learning to ride their new bicycles with the help of training wheels. Martin started them on the sidewalk as he trailed behind them so that they were able to land on the lawns when they took an occasional spill.

With the new year, Belle Hoskins started her pupils on Bach's "Well-Tempered Clavier," a famous collection of preludes and fugues. Martin never had to remind them to practice. They each spent at least an hour a day at the piano. Periodic recitals added to their incentive to practice.

School seemed to be going well for them until one day when they came home looking upset. Martin pressed them to tell him what was wrong. They seemed reluctant to tell him, but eventually Minnie opened up.

"Last week we had a spell-down with the sixth-graders. We were the last two left standing after Samantha missed on 'asphyxiate.' She was embarrassed because she usually won. Later she asked me what my father did for a living, and I told her I didn't know. She said that made us bastards. I had to look it up. It means..."

"I know what it means," said Martin, trying to conceal his anger. "Nobody should use that word. It's a remnant of a different time. You're just as good as any of them. Don't ever forget that."

That seemed to mollify them for the moment, but Martin sensed that he would have to address the issue again in more detail. He decided to wait until Angela's next visit. She was much better than he at dealing with social issues.

✦

The next day Martin called Angela and told her what had happened. She was there by the time the twins got home from school. After the two had had a snack and a glass of milk, they all sat down in the living room. Martin was only too glad to let Angela begin.

"How much do you know about human reproduction?" she asked, clearly recognizing that there was no need to talk to them in childish terms.

Max looked at Minnie, then at Angela, and said, "We know where babies come from."

But since they didn't seem to know how they got there, Angela explained the process in simple, non-clinical terms.

Then she added, "In most cases, married people have

babies. But sometimes, people who aren't married have babies. When that happens, it isn't always the parents who care for the children. Sometimes the mother does it alone. Sometimes the grandparents are involved. Sometimes foster parents or adoptive parents take care of them."

"And sometimes the great uncle does it," said Max.

"Right. But no matter who rears the children, they are no less important than any others. And sometimes they're better off."

Minnie turned to Martin and asked, "Do you know who our father is?"

Martin shook his head and said, "No. I doubt if we will ever know. Someone took advantage of your mother while she was unconscious. He couldn't even know about you."

"So we really are bastards," said Max.

"We don't use that term anymore," replied Angela. "Even the word 'illegitimate' is less common. Someone observed that there are no illegitimate children, only illegitimate parents. None of us had any control over the circumstances of our birth."

Martin added, "Don't be too hard on your mother, either. She did the best she could for you. And she still cares about you."

Minnie asked, "What do we say when the other kids bring it up?"

Martin replied, "Don't say anything. You don't owe them an explanation. It's none of their business."

Angela added, "I don't want you to feel that the

circumstances of your birth make you inferior in any way. Here's something for you to think about. Have you ever heard of Leonardo Da Vinci?"

The twins nodded and Minnie said, "He painted the Mona Lisa."

Angela continued, "My people came from Italy, and he was one of the most famous Italians who ever lived. He was an absolute genius, not just a great artist. And I'll tell you something else about him. Da Vinci was not his surname. He didn't have one. His name was just Leonardo, and he came from the town of Vinci. His parents weren't married. But nobody calls him a bastard. The conditions of his birth are unimportant. And so are yours. You have a family, even if it's unconventional, and you have unlimited opportunity. Down the road, nobody will particularly care who your father was, and it would be a waste of time for you to speculate on it. It will be up to you to take advantage of the opportunities you've been given and make something of yourselves."

Each twin showed a trace of a smile, and Minnie said, "Thank you."

Angela said, "Now give me hugs and play something for me."

19

A mild winter gave way to an early spring. The twins became proficient at riding their bicycles on the sidewalk. Soon they would be ready for the pavement. Martin's anxiety was relieved somewhat by the lack of heavy traffic on their street. Still, he drilled them thoroughly on safety procedures.

A piano recital in February was poorly attended, but Mr. Sterling asked the twins to play some of the Bach preludes for the next PTA meeting. Many of the parents and all of the teachers were aware by then that the two possessed exceptional musical talent. Soon requests were coming in for the two to play for other events, most of which included a modest payment. For the first time in their young lives, the youngsters had their own spending money, but Martin insisted that they open savings accounts.

With March came their birthdays. They turned ten on the third of March. Martin asked them if they wanted to celebrate the occasion with their class, but they were reluctant to emphasize the fact that they were younger than any of the others. They just wanted to invite Angela. She accepted and even offered to provide ice cream and a birthday cake. Martin bought them bicycle helmets and more CDs. Angela gave them an encyclopedia of famous composers. Both of them deferred a request for a puppy.

When the time came for Angela to leave, the twins hugged her and thanked her for the treats and the book. Then Minnie surprised her by saying, "I wish you could stay here with us. You're like part of our family."

Max nodded affirmatively, but didn't say anything. Martin didn't know what to say at first, but as he hugged Angela, he said, "Maybe we should discuss this."

She responded simply with a smile and a kiss on the cheek.

A few days later, Jewel called Martin. She was all excited.

"I'm getting out next month! I'll be paroled for the rest of my sentence, and I'll have to live in a half-way house for the first few months, but at least I won't be locked up. I'll even have a job. I'll be working in the accounting department at a Sears store."

"That's great!" Martin replied. "Here's your chance to turn your life around."

"Yeah. And don't worry. I know a good deal when I see it. I won't blow it."

"I'm betting on you," said Martin. "As I told you, I'll help you in any way I can."

"Thanks a lot," she said. "I'll let you know. They'll help me get set up, though. They don't just unlock the door and turn us loose."

"Good. Just keep me informed. Whenever you're ready, I'll bring the twins to see you."

"I really want to see them," she said, "but let's wait until I'm out of the half-way house."

"That will be summer, and it will be easier to get away then. We won't have school schedules to deal with."

"That should work out better," she said. "Can I say 'hi' to them before I have to hang up?"

"Sure. Here's Max."

Once again, the twins showed little expression as they spoke briefly with their mother.

20

One day in the middle of March Minnie mentioned over supper that they were studying the history and geography of Nebraska in school. Both she and Max felt that they were at a disadvantage because they had only seen the area in and around Omaha. It only took Martin a minute to formulate a solution.

"During this time of the year, central Nebraska is the site of a massive migration of geese and sandhill cranes. We could take a weekend trip on Interstate 80 to see them and expose you to more of our state. The interstate follows the Platte River as far as the cities of North Platte and Ogallala, and that is what attracts the birds. It's the only major source of surface water for much of the state."

As usual, the twins looked at each other before responding. Then Max said, "We'd like that. We've hardly been anywhere away from home."

Martin found the thought sobering that a two-day trip

would constitute the longest journey that the two children had ever taken in their ten years.

"All right, then," he said. "We'll go next weekend. We'll follow the Platte River to Ogallala, spend the night in a motel, and come back by a different route. That will give you a fair idea of what Nebraska looks like. It isn't very scenic, especially at this time of the year, but watching the birds will add some color and interest."

Minnie commented, "We've only driven across Illinois and Iowa, and they weren't very scenic either."

Martin smiled and said, "This summer we'll have to find some scenery. Maybe we'll go to a national park."

"I'd like to see Yellowstone Park," said Max.

"I want to see the Grand Canyon," added Minnie.

"What? No Disneyland?" Martin asked.

"Naw," said Max. "That's kid stuff."

The next Saturday the three ate breakfast and headed out. Martin had asked Angela to join them, but the demands of her job precluded an absence at that particular time.

As they drove south toward Lincoln, Martin asked the children to tell him what they had learned in school about the route they were taking.

Minnie began, "Omaha is the largest city in Nebraska. It's named for an Indian tribe. But it isn't the capital. That's Lincoln, which is named for President Abraham Lincoln. It's the second-largest city."

Martin added, "Some say that on home football Saturdays, the stadium at the University of Nebraska is the third-largest city in the state."

It took the twins a moment to grasp that observation.

The traffic on the interstate was heavy as they left Omaha and remained that way for the first part of the journey. The truck traffic was particularly noticeable.

When they crossed the Platte River just south of Omaha, it was Max's turn to recite. "The North Platte River forms in the mountains of Colorado, flows to the north into Wyoming, joins the smaller South Platte River in western Nebraska, then runs eastward across Nebraska until it reaches the Missouri River just south of Omaha. There are dams on the North Platte River in Wyoming and Nebraska. The biggest one is near Ogallala, where it forms a reservoir over twenty miles long. It's called Lake McConaughy. The main purpose of the dams is to make sure that there is plenty of water for irrigation when it doesn't rain much."

"You'll see the dam and the reservoir today," said Martin. "They're pretty impressive. But you'll notice that the river isn't very impressive. It tends to be shallow and muddy, not suitable for navigation. However, it has played an important role in the development of this region."

"I know," said Minnie. "The Pony Express and the Oregon Trail followed it, and then after the Civil War the railroad followed it."

"Right," replied Martin. "Most of the towns we'll be passing were located there because of the railroad. This is a major agricultural area, and the people needed the railroad to ship their grain and cattle back east. When the highways were built, the Lincoln Highway ran parallel to the rails across Nebraska. It was only about fifty years ago that it was largely replaced by Interstate 80."

As they passed the exits for Grand Island, Kearney, and smaller towns, Martin tried to explain the significance of each as best he could. Just east of Kearney there was a large archway extending across the highway. "This is a frontier and Native American museum," he said. "It wasn't here the last time I came this way. We won't have time to stop there this trip, but maybe next time we'll plan to visit it."

By then they were starting to see small flocks of snow geese and sandhill cranes. They stopped in Kearney for a bite to eat before continuing their journey.

As they drove westward, Martin offered his interpretation of the vast migration of large birds. "The white geese and the darker ones are closely related. The darker ones are called blue geese, even though they aren't really blue. The larger ones are called Canada geese. A lot of the geese will fly up to Canada to nest. The long-legged birds over there are sandhill cranes. Northern Nebraska has a lot of sand hills which are not well suited for agriculture. The cranes get their name from that region."

As they continued their journey, they saw some ponds that were nearly all white with snow geese, and some of the fields were covered with hundreds of sandhill cranes. Meanwhile, the sky was full of geese, cranes, and a few ducks. It was an awesome display of nature.

Martin explained, "If we were to take this trip a month from now, we probably wouldn't see any of these birds.

They would be up north nesting by then. They congregate here every spring on their way north just because of the Platte River. It's like an oasis to them. There isn't much water on either side of it."

The twins were intrigued by the avian panorama. There seemed to be no end to the flocks of geese and cranes for about two hundred miles.

Just before they reached the North Platte exits, they saw signs for the Buffalo Bill ranch.

Martin asked if they knew who Buffalo Bill was.

Max replied, "He was a famous wild west character. I think he ran a western show when he was older."

"Right," said Martin. "He toured this country and Europe with a show featuring cowboys and Indians. Annie Oakley and Chief Sitting Bull were among the stars. After he and his wife died, they were buried on a mountain top west of Denver. Lots of tourists visit their graves."

When they reached the North Platte exit, Martin had another story to tell. "The city of North Platte is a major center for the Union Pacific Railroad. During World War II it became the site of a very unique operation. Some of the local people noticed that troop trains were stopping there every day carrying soldiers and sailors destined for the European or Pacific war zones. Some of the women in the area decided to provide coffee and sandwiches or pastry for the thousands of servicemen on the trains. At a time when sugar and gasoline were strictly rationed, they managed to meet every train with their home-made snacks. They kept it up for months. It's one of those stories which help restore your faith in the human race.

At the same time that some people were doing horrible things to others, a group of women here was doing exactly the opposite. Somebody wrote a book about it. I'm glad, because everyone should know about it."

✦

As they drove the fifty-mile stretch between North Platte and Ogallala, Minnie commented on a sign which indicated that they were making the transition from Central Standard to Mountain Standard Time. Martin observed, "You two have spent your whole lives on Central Standard Time. This will be your first experience with a different time zone. We just gained an hour. But we'll lose it tomorrow when we return this way. It's just a way of keeping up with the rotation of the earth. But it poses a bit of a problem for the people who commute between North Platte and Ogallala. They have to deal with two time zones every day."

Max reflected, "I suppose they just stay adjusted to one and try to ignore the other. That's what I'd do."

Martin smiled at the practical wisdom of a ten-year-old. Then he tried to give them some information about Ogallala.

"Ogallala is named for a branch of the Sioux or Lakota tribe. It has several claims to fame. It is near the location of a big dam on the North Platte River, as I mentioned. I remember seeing a sign here which read, 'Ogallala: Best town by a dam site.'" He paused for a moment to let them catch the pun, then continued. "But there is another connection with water for which Ogallala is famous. There is an enormous underground reservoir which extends all the way from South Dakota to Texas. I'm not sure why, but it's called the Ogallala aquifer. Maybe it's because Ogallala lies toward the northern extreme, and there aren't many larger cities over it. Because of the heavy demand for water, the aquifer is shrinking. Most of the land above it receives too little rain, and many of the people there are dependent on sub-soil water, especially for agriculture. Farmers all over the West who don't irrigate can expect to lose their crops periodically. As the population grows, the demand for water increases accordingly. Your generation will have to deal with that more than ever before."

The twins had no response to that sobering assessment.

As they approached Ogallala, they saw a sign which read, "Where the West begins." Martin commented, "Interstate 80 continues all the way to California, but it parts company with the North Platte River from here on except to cross it in Wyoming. That means that our bird show won't continue very far west of here. After we've lined up a motel room, we'll drive up to the dam and have a look at it and Lake McConaughy. During the summer there's a western stage show here, but it won't have started yet. We'll have to find something else to do."

Max commented, "We're not seeing as many plowed fields as there were farther east. Why is that?"

Martin smiled and replied, "You're very observant. We've been steadily climbing as we've driven westward. Higher elevation means a shorter growing season. It also means that the topsoil has been washing downhill for centuries. The eastern slope of the Rocky Mountains is actually a high desert which extends about this far eastward. With high elevation, unfertile soil, and minimal rainfall, it has limited suitability for agriculture. Most of the land is used for grazing livestock, and some of it is not even very useful for that."

Minnie asked, "Does that mean that eastern Nebraska is mostly farmland and western Nebraska is pasture for animals?"

"Not quite," Martin replied. "Much of northern Nebraska is sandy and less suited for agriculture, and the northwestern corner starts to look more like the Black Hills of South Dakota. This may be called the Cornhusker State, but it's really more complex than that."

Max said, "I'm really glad we took this trip. If we're going to be Nebraskans, then at least we'll have some idea what that means."

"I'm glad we did this, too," said Martin. "I hadn't been out here in a long time. It's good to re-connect."

When they reached the first Ogallala turn-off, Martin took it and located a motel, where he checked in. Then they drove a few miles north to the dam. It was getting chilly when they got out and looked at the big barrier with water stretching back farther than they could see. Martin tried to summarize the scene.

"This reservoir provides recreation and camping sites for a lot of people in the area. It also provides drinking water, bath water, and irrigation for many. Water running through turbines in the dam also provides electricity for a big area. It's quite a project."

It was too chilly for them to stay there for long, and so they returned to Ogallala, ate an early supper, and watched a TV movie in their motel room.

The next morning they left the motel, ate breakfast in a café, and started back. They followed the interstate highway as far as Lexington, then drove north to Broken Bow. There they picked up Highway 32, which took them all the way back to Omaha. The two-lane highway was slower than the interstate, but it was more relaxing because of the reduced traffic. As they drove from one town to another, they pointed out whatever caught their attention. After a lunch break, they continued to Omaha, arriving there by late afternoon. Martin used his cell phone for the first time to call Angela from the outskirts and let her know that they were back.

21

March went out like the proverbial lamb, and April made its debut with more sunshine than showers. Martin raked his yard and was delighted to see small flowers emerging from under the dead leaves. He started making plans for his garden.

As he sent the twins off to school one day, he reflected on how little they resembled the bedraggled urchins who had arrived the previous summer. They were well adjusted in school, improving their physical skills, and dazzling everyone who heard their piano playing. Martin felt justified in taking pride in his part of their development.

With Easter approaching, Martin decided that it would be a good time to buy the twins some new dress clothes, mainly because they were outgrowing the old ones. Before long he would have to replace everything. This time he felt secure enough to shop without relying on Alice for support.

On Easter Sunday they were joined by Angela for the church service, and then they all went to the Flannigan home for a traditional ham dinner. It occurred to Martin that Angela was now being routinely included in their activities, whether he mentioned her or not. At one point, Alice drew him aside and asked him bluntly, "When are you going to marry that woman?"

Martin pretended to look startled and replied innocently, "Why, she hasn't asked me yet."

Alice just grinned.

On a Saturday afternoon in May there was a highly unusual wedding ceremony at the Presbyterian Church. The groom was fifty-nine years old, the bride was forty-seven, and the two attendants were ten. The only witnesses were the pastor's wife, Belle Hoskins and her husband, and the Flannigans. After the simple ceremony, the small group went to a local restaurant for supper, then they all went home.

Since Angela had been living in a furnished apartment, there was relatively little to move. Martin and Mike had transported most of it that morning. They could take their time with the rest.

It seemed appropriate to include the twins in what passed for a honeymoon a month later, since they were such an integral part of the marriage. They were family.

22

The next year passed quickly as the new family made the necessary adjustments. Martin and Angela had both lived alone for so long that the concept of compromise was rather novel, but the situation improved with time. Martin fulfilled the first phase of his promise by taking the family to the Black Hills and Mount Rushmore in June. Neither of the twins showed any sign of losing interest in music. They played increasingly complex piano pieces as the spans of their hands grew into them and their feet reached the pedals. They completed the sixth grade and were accepted into the honors program at a public junior high school. As they turned eleven, Minnie began to show signs of puberty before her brother, which was typical for a female, but they remained close and shared secrets. The only dark cloud on the horizon was Jewel's situation.

↜↝

As previously agreed, Martin had waited until Jewel was released from the half-way house to bring the children to see her. Angela had some reservations about coming along, but Martin assured her that she was too much a part of the situation to avoid any of it. By the time of their visit, Jewel had been working at Sears for six months and had just moved into an apartment. On a fall Saturday they made the drive to Peoria, checked into a motel, and located Jewel's apartment house. She had told Martin what time she would be home from work, and so they were able to time their arrival accordingly. Her small furnished apartment was on the third floor of a twelve-unit building in a working-class neighborhood. She looked quite nervous as she opened the door, but she hugged each of the visitors and tried to look calm. Since she had not seen the twins in nearly two years, she remarked on their growth. They were nearly as tall as she. It was nearly supper time, but she offered them each a glass of lemonade. They would be going out for supper. Angela speculated that Jewel's culinary skills were probably not up to preparing supper for five. She said very little during the visit, preferring to act as a silent observer.

Over supper and afterward in the apartment, Jewel asked the twins many questions. At first they seemed apprehensive about her, but they gradually loosened up and told her about their activities. Then she told them about her situation. Her accounting job had been difficult for her at first, but she was becoming more comfortable with it. She had taken a driver's education course and bought a used Chevy with some of the money which

Martin had sent her from her parents' estate. Little by little she was making the transition. Two of her co-workers had been particularly helpful, and no one had made any reference to her past.

The evening passed quickly, and the guests prepared to leave for their motel. Just before they left, Jewel took Martin aside and said, "I still haven't given up hope that my children will come back to me some day, but I don't know when that can happen. I'm really glad to hear them call your wife 'Aunt Angela.' It would have devastated me to hear them call her 'Mom.'"

Martin found the remark disturbing, but decided not to say anything about it. It had never occurred to him that Jewel would ever presume to ask for custody of her children.

Just before they left, Angela asked Jewel, "Since you're free to travel now, would you like to visit us around Christmas?"

Jewel quickly responded, "That would be a bad time for me. Sears and all the other big stores are especially busy just before Christmas."

"Then we'll try to pay you another visit when it's more convenient for you," said Angela.

"That would be nice," Jewel replied. She hugged Martin and Angela and kissed the children. Their response was polite but less than enthusiastic.

As they drove home the next day, Angela asked the children for their reaction to the visit. Max said, "I don't feel that I really know her."

Minnie followed, "She was gone a lot when we lived with her. We don't have many good memories of her."

Martin silently hoped that he would never have to get into a custody battle with Jewel.

+~+

The weekend before Christmas the four made another trip to Peoria. It was snowing lightly, but the roads were still clear. The forecast looked favorable for the return trip.

This time Jewel would not be alone. She had been dating another Sears employee named Donald Graf and wanted them to meet him. He was a pleasant-looking man who appeared to be in his late thirties. Again they went out to supper, but this time Donald picked up the check. When they returned to the apartment, the conversation flowed freely, and Jewel seemed more relaxed. Nobody mentioned whether Donald had been married, and it seemed improper to ask. By the end of the evening, it seemed as if several questions had remained unasked, such as how much Donald knew about Jewel's past. Most of the conversation focused on the children. It seemed rather incongruous for Jewel to be trying to show them off to her new boyfriend when she had had so little to do with their development. Martin and Angela left with mixed feelings about their visit. Again the twins had little to say about it.

+~+

When Martin tried to arrange for Jewel to visit them over the children's spring break, he received a surprising reason why she would be unable to come. She and Donald had just gotten married and were going on their honeymoon to Florida. She apologized for not inviting Martin and his family to the wedding, but they had done it on short notice with no fanfare. She had just moved into his house, but had kept her telephone number.

Martin was too surprised to make an immediate comment other than "congratulations!" After he had collected his thoughts, he reminded her that the twins would be completing their schooling at Halley's and would be participating in a commencement program in May. That would be an appropriate time for Jewel and Donald to come.

"Do you remember our house?" he asked. "You were here once with your parents as a child."

"Vaguely," she replied. "I remember that Aunt Eloise was a really good cook. I couldn't tell anyone how to find your house, though."

"I'll give you directions. We'll find a place for you and Donald to stay."

"All right. We'll plan to be there."

On a cool day in May, Halley School for Gifted Children held its commencement service in recognition of fourteen exceptional children. The highlight of the program was a piano duet performed by Max and Minnie

Bradley. Jewel and Donald were awed by the talent displayed by the two youngsters. Mike and Alice Flannigan, who had provided a bedroom for Jewel and Donald during their stay, were also there. All of them were duly impressed with the accomplishments of such young children.

After the service, they all went to the Bradley home for a barbeque. Donald seemed comfortable with his unorthodox new family and their friends. He chatted amiably with everyone and even tried telling some jokes.

While Martin was outside attending the grill, Jewel came to him.

"I want to tell you something, Uncle Martin," she said. "I've been thinking about this a lot, and I've discussed it with Donald. He has two children by his first marriage and has them twice a month. As much as I'd like to have mine back, I realize that they're much better off with you and Angela. If it's all right with you, I'd like to see them fairly often, but not try to get in their way. I hope they won't think too badly of me."

Martin tried not to show his relief and replied, "Sometimes the best thing we can do for our children is to let them go. One day I'll have to let them go, too."

Jewel was teary-eyed and didn't trust her voice to say any more, so she just smiled.

Breinigsville, PA USA
16 July 2010
241876BV00004B/8/P